The Clockmaker

Georges Simenon

THE CLOCKMAKER

Translated by Norman Denny

Originally published in English as "The Watchmaker"

A HARVEST/HBJ BOOK

A Helen and Kurt Wolff Book
Harcourt Brace Jovanovich
New York and London

Printed in the United States of America

Translation reprinted by permission of Doubleday & Company, Inc.

Library of Congress Cataloging in Publication Data

Simenon, Georges, 1903–
The clockmaker.

(A Harvest/HBJ book)
Translation of L'Horloger d'Everton.
Reprinted from the 1967 ed. of a collection of the author's stories which were
issued under title: An American omnibus.
"A Helen and Kurt Wolff book."
I. Title.
[PZ3.S5892C 3]   [PQ2637.I53]   843'.9'12   77-4646
ISBN 0-15-618170-3 pbk.

First Harvest/HBJ edition 1977

A B C D E F G H I J

The Clockmaker

Until midnight, actually until one o'clock in the morning, he followed the routine of every evening, or more exactly of Saturdays, which were a little different from other days.

Would he have spent that evening differently, or would he have tried to enjoy it more, if he had foreseen that it was his last evening as a happy man? To this question and many others, including that of whether he had ever been really happy, he would later have to try to find an answer.

As yet he knew nothing of it, and contented himself with living, without haste, without problems, without even being fully conscious of living them, hours so similar to others that he might have thought he had already lived them.

It rarely happened that he shut the shop at six o'clock precisely. Nearly always he let a few more minutes pass before getting up from his workbench, in front of which the watches under repair hung from little hooks, and removing from his right eye the magnifying glass, framed in black ebonite, which he wore nearly all day like a monocle. Perhaps, even after years, he still had a sense of working for an employer and was afraid of seeming to grudge his time.

3

Mrs. Pinch next door, who kept the real-estate agency, closed at five o'clock sharp. The hairdresser on the other side, for fear of being late, began to refuse customers at half-past five, and Galloway, at the moment of opening his display window, nearly always saw him getting into his car to drive home. The hairdresser had a nice house in the residential quarter, on the hill, and three children at school.

In a few minutes, moving with the precise, rather slow gestures of a man accustomed to handling delicate and valuable objects, Dave Galloway cleared the display shelves of their watches and jewels, which he stored away in the safe at the back of the shop.

The most expensive watches were worth not quite a hundred dollars. The others were very much cheaper. All the jewels were in plated settings, with imitation stones. He had tried at first to sell engagement rings adorned with a real diamond, a diamond of about a half carat, but for purchases of this sort the Everton people preferred to go to Poughkeepsie or even to New York, perhaps because it would have embarrassed them to buy their engagement rings by monthly installments from someone they knew.

He put the contents of the till in a drawer in the safe, took off his unbleached working smock, which he hung on a hook on the inside of the door of the cupboard, put on his jacket, and glanced around to see that everything was in order.

It was May; the sun was still quite high in a sky of very soft blue, and all day long the air had been motionless.

When he had slipped the spring lock of the door and gone out, he glanced automatically toward the movie house, the Colonial Theater, whose neon sign had just lighted up, although it was still broad daylight. The same thing happened every Saturday, because of the seven-o'clock performance. There was a lawn in front of the theater, a few linden trees on which the leaves scarcely stirred.

Standing on his doorstep, Galloway lit a cigarette, one of the five or six he smoked in a day, then walked slowly around the long building of which the ground floor was occupied by shops.

He lived on the second floor, exactly over his own shop, but since there was no communication between the latter and his apartment, he had to turn to the left past the hairdresser's establishment, go around to the back, where the entrance to the apartments was situated.

As happened nearly every Saturday, his son had come in during the afternoon to say that he would not be home for dinner. No doubt he would get a hot dog or a sandwich somewhere, probably at Mack's Lunch.

Galloway went upstairs, turned the key in the lock, and went at once to open the window, from which he had almost exactly the same view as from his workbench, with the same trees, the movie house, whose lights, in the full sunshine, were out of place, almost disturbing.

He no longer noticed that every day he went through the same motions, in the same order, and that it was this, perhaps, that gave him so peaceful and reassuring an aspect. Nothing was left lying about in the kitchen, where he always washed up after the midday meal before going downstairs again. He knew what cold meat he would find in the refrigerator and precisely where, and he handled the objects as though by magic; his place was very quickly set, with the glass of water, the bread, the butter, the coffee beginning to bubble in the percolator.

When he was alone, he read while he ate, but this did not prevent him from hearing the birds in the trees, or the noise of a car someone was starting, which he recognized. From his seat he could even see the youngsters beginning to move toward the Colonial, which they would not enter until the last minute.

He drank his coffee in little sips, washed up, cleared away the bread crumbs. So far as his activities and movements were concerned, nothing unusual took place and shortly before seven, he was out in the street again, greeted the garageman, who with his wife was on the way to the movies.

He saw some young boys and girls in the distance, did not spot Ben, did not try to meet him, knowing that the boy did not like him to seem to be keeping an eye on him.

It was not really a matter of keeping an eye on him, as Ben knew. If sometimes his father went out of his way to catch a glimpse of him, it was not in order to supervise his actions and behavior, but simply for the pleasure of making contact with him, even at a distance. A boy of sixteen can't understand this. It was natural that, when he was with boys and girls of his own age, Ben should prefer his father not to be watching. The matter had never been referred to between them.

The building in which he had his shop and apartment was nearly on the corner of Main Street; along it he now went, past the drugstore, which stayed open till nine, then the post office with its white columns, then the newspaper store. Cars went by, scarcely slowing, some not slowing at all, as though they did not notice they were passing through a village.

Beyond the gasoline pump, scarcely a quarter of a mile from his own house, he turned to the right into a street bordered with trees, where the white houses were surrounded by lawns. This street did not lead anywhere, and the only cars to be seen on it were those belonging to its inhabitants. All the windows were open, children were still playing out of doors, men without jackets, their shirt sleeves rolled up, were driving motor mowers over the lawns.

Every year brought similar evenings of this almost oppressive mildness and the hum of mowers, just as every autumn brought the sound of rakes on the dead leaves and the smell of these leaves being burned, in the evening, in front of the houses, and later still there was inevitably the scraping of shovels on the hardened snow.

From time to time, with a gesture or a word, he returned a "Good evening."

On Tuesdays he also went out, to go to the town hall for the meeting of the School Committee, of which he was secretary.

On other evenings, except Saturday, he most often stayed at home, reading or watching television.

Saturday was the evening for Musak, who must at that moment be awaiting him in one of the rocking chairs on his porch.

His house, built of wood, like the other houses in the neighborhood, was the last of the row, backing onto a steep slope, so that what was the second floor on one side became the ground floor on the other. It was painted pale yellow instead of white, and less than fifty yards away was a stretch of wasteland where people were in the habit of dumping anything they wanted to get rid of, iron bedsteads, broken-down baby carriages, split metal drums.

From the terrace one looked over the sports field, where, every evening in summer, the baseball team practiced.

The two men treated each other without ceremony. Galloway could not remember ever having shaken hands with Musak, who, when he arrived, contented himself with uttering a grunt and pointing toward the second rocking chair.

It was the same that evening as on other Saturdays. They followed at a distance the white uniforms of the players against the steadily darkening green of the field, and they heard their cries, the whistle of the coach, who was very fat and worked during the day behind one of the counters of the hardware store.

"Nice evening" was all Galloway had said after sitting down.

A little later Musak had grumbled:

"If they don't make up their minds to change their damned pitcher we'll be at the bottom of the list again at the end of the season."

Musak talked in a surly voice no matter what he said, and it was rare for him to smile. In fact Dave Galloway could not remember ever having seen him smile. What he sometimes did was to burst into a loud laugh that must have alarmed those who did not know him.

In the village people were no longer alarmed by Musak because they had grown used to him. Elsewhere he ran the risk of being taken for one of those elderly convicts broken out of jail whose photographs, full-face and in profile, are to be seen in post offices above the notice, "Wanted."

Galloway, who did not know his age, would never have thought of asking him what it was any more than he would have asked what European country he had come from when he was still just a child. He knew only that he had made the crossing in an immigrant ship with his father, his mother, and five or six brothers and sisters, and that they had first lived on the outskirts of Philadelphia. What had become of the brothers and sisters? The subject had never been mentioned between them, or what Musak had done before settling all alone in Everton twenty years ago.

He must have been married, because he had a daughter somewhere in Southern California, who wrote to him from time to time and sent him photographs of her children. She had never been to see him. He had never gone out there, either.

Was Musak divorced, or a widower?

At some period in his life he had worked in a piano factory—this was all Galloway knew—and he had had enough money, when he came to Everton, to be able to buy a house.

He was probably sixty, or even older. Some people claimed that he was in his seventies, which wasn't impossible either.

He still worked from morning till night in the workshop behind the house, on the side where the second floor became the ground floor, so that the workshop communicated directly with his bedroom. This was where they often sat in the winter, when they could not sit on the porch. Musak would finish some job or other, always a delicate one, with hands so large that one might have thought them clumsy. There was an iron stove in the middle of the room, which was cluttered up with workbenches, glue heating in a pot of water, wood shavings on the floor.

His specialty was doing work that called for extreme patience, repairing old furniture or old clock cases, or making small, elaborate articles, boxes inlaid with mahogany or woods from the West Indies.

They could remain for a long time without talking, the two of them, satisfied to be there watching at a distance the players running back and forth while the sun sank slowly behind the trees and the air little by little became the same blue as the sky.

For Dave Galloway what characterized the winter evenings in the workshop was the smell of wood shavings mingled with that of strong glue.

In the summer evenings, on the porch, there was another smell, equally recognizable, that of the pipe that Musak smoked in small puffs. He must have adopted some special tobacco, which had an acrid and yet not unpleasant smell. It came to Galloway in waves at the same time as that of the grass cut in the neighboring gardens. Musak's garments were impregnated with it, his very body, one could have sworn, smelled of the pipe, and also the living room of his house.

Why had he, so adroit with his hands, so meticulous in everything he undertook, been content to mend his favorite pipe with a piece of wire? A little air passed through the crack each time he sucked and it made a queer sound, like the breathing of certain sick people.

"Who are they playing tomorrow?"

"Radley."

"They'll get licked."

There was a baseball game every Sunday and Galloway sat on the benches while old Musak contented himself with watching from his porch. He had astonishingly good eyesight. From that distance he could recognize every player and, on the Sunday evening, could have given a list of all the local people who had watched the game.

The movements on the field grew slower, the voices less piercing, the referee's blasts of the whistle more infrequent. They could scarcely see the ball any longer in the half-light and a certain freshness began to prevail; one would have said that the air, hitherto motionless, was awakening at the approach of night.

Perhaps both men were equally impatient to go indoors and begin their Saturday-night pastime, but, as though of one accord, they awaited the signal; neither of them moved before all the figures in baseball clothes had gathered together in a corner of the field to hear the comments of the coach.

By that time the darkness was almost complete. The radios were growing more strident in the neighboring houses, some windows were lighting up, others, because of television, remained in obscurity.

Only then did they look at one another and one seemed to say: "Shall we go?"

Theirs was a strange friendship. Galloway could not have said, any more than Musak, how it had begun, and they seemed to take no account of the twenty years that separated them.

"If I remember rightly, I have to get my revenge."

It was the cabinetmaker's only fault: he did not like losing. He did not get angry, never thumped the table with his fist. As a rule he said nothing, but his face became sulky, like that of a child, and sometimes, after an evening when he had been badly beaten, he would go two or three days without seeming to see Galloway when he passed him in the street.

He turned on the light and they entered another atmosphere even quieter, more enveloping than that which they had left. The living room was comfortable, as well cared for as by any woman, with handsome furniture carefully polished, and Galloway had never detected in it the slightest disorder.

The backgammon board was ready on a low table, always in the same place, between the same armchairs, with a floor lamp, which shone on it, and they liked to leave the rest of the room in the shadow where only reflections existed.

The bottle of rye was also in readiness, and the glasses, and there was nothing more to be done, before beginning the game, except to go and bring ice from the kitchen.

"Your health."

"And yours."

Galloway drank little, two glasses at the most during the evening, whereas Musak took five or six without their seeming to have the least effect on him.

Each threw the dice.

"Six! I begin."

For nearly two hours their lives were attuned to the rhythm of the falling dice and the sound of the yellow and black pieces. The pipe made its whistling noise. Its acrid scent gradually enveloped Galloway. At long intervals one of the two uttered a remark such as:

"John Duncan bought a new car."

Or:

"They say Mrs. Pinch has sold Meadow Farm for fifty thousand dollars."

These called for no reply. These prompted neither question nor comment.

They played until half-past eleven, which was about their limit. Musak lost the first game, won three others, which averaged out with the previous time.

"I said I'd beat you! I only lose when I can't bring myself to concentrate. A nightcap?"

"No, thanks."

The cabinetmaker poured himself one, and this drink he always took neat. Also, toward the end of the contest, his breathing always became noisy, his nose made almost the same sound as his pipe. He must have snored at nights, which would not disturb anyone, since he lived alone in the house.

Did he wash the glasses before going to bed?

"Good night."

"Good night."

"Still pleased with your son?"

"Very pleased."

Galloway felt uncomfortable whenever Musak asked in this fashion after Ben. He was convinced that his friend was not malicious, still less cruel, and had no reason to be jealous of him. Perhaps, in any case, he was imagining things? One would have said that it ruffled Musak that Ben should be a well-behaved boy of whom his father had never had reason to complain.

Had he once had difficulties with his daughter? Or was he sorry that he had not had a son as well?

There was something different in his voice, in his look, when he touched upon that subject. He seemed to be saying:

"All right! All right! We shall see how long it lasts!"

Or again did he suspect Galloway of deceiving himself about his son?

"He's not playing baseball any more?"

"Not this year."

Last year Ben had been one of the best players in the high-school team. This year suddenly he had decided not to play. He had not given any reason. His father had not asked. Wasn't it the same with all youngsters? One year they are crazy about a game or a sport, and the next year they don't talk about it any more. For months they meet the same group of friends every day, and then one day they break away from them for no apparent reason to join another group.

Galloway, needless to say, would have preferred it to be otherwise. He was greatly distressed when Ben gave up baseball, because his greatest pleasure had been to watch the school games, even when the team traveled thirty or forty miles to play on some other field.

"No doubt he's a good boy," said Musak.

Why did he say it with an air of concluding an argument, of putting a full stop to the conversation? What exactly did the words signify?

Perhaps Dave Galloway was too touchy where Ben was concerned? It was natural for people to ask:

"How's your son getting on?"

Or again:

"It's a long time since I saw Ben."

He had a tendency to look for some special significance in these passing remarks.

"I've no reason to complain of him," he most commonly replied.

And it was true. He could formulate no complaint. Ben had never caused him any trouble. They never quarreled. It was rare for Galloway to have to reprimand his son, and when it happened he did so quietly, as man to man.

"Good night."

"Good night."

"Till Saturday."

"Yes."

They saw each other a dozen times during the week, notably at the post office, where they both went almost every day at the same time to collect their mail. Galloway had a card that he hung on his door whenever he had to be away, or to go up to his apartment—"Back soon."

They also met at the garage and at the news dealer's. Nevertheless, when they separated on Saturday nights they invariably said:

"Till Saturday."

The tobacco's bitter smell followed Galloway for a dozen yards, and as he went toward Main Street, where nearly all the lights were out, he heard, in two of the houses only, the echoes of the same boxing match.

Did it take him six minutes to return home? Scarcely. Nothing remained open, at the end of the village, except the Old Barn Tavern, with its red and green lights that, even at a distance, made one think of brands of beer and whisky.

He walked around his building, and only as he was entering the alleyway, past the hairdresser's shop, did it occur to him that he had not seen any light in his window.

He did not remember raising his head, either, but he was sure he had done so because he always did so, with a mechanical movement, when he returned home in the evening. He was so accustomed to seeing the lighted window that he no longer thought about it.

But now, as he went toward the stairs, he could have sworn that the window was in darkness. There was no dance that night, no party, nothing special to keep Ben out late.

He started up the stairs and after going a few steps he knew, without the possibility of error, that there had been no light in the apartment, because he would have seen a streak under the door.

Had Ben come in early and gone to bed? Who knows? Perhaps he hadn't been feeling well.

He turned the key in the lock, called as he pushed open the door:

"Ben!"

The echo of his own voice in the room told him that there was no one there, but he would not admit it, turned on the light in the living room, went toward his son's room, repeating in a voice as normal as possible:

"Ben!"

He must show no anxiety because, if Ben were there, if he were really in bed, would he not look at him in annoyed surprise as he asked:

"What's the matter?"

There was nothing the matter, of course. Nothing could be the matter. One must never let one's fears be seen, especially by a boy in the process of becoming a man.

"Are you there?"

He tried to smile in advance, as though his son were watching him.

But Ben was not there. The room was empty. The bed was untouched.

Perhaps he had left a note on the table, as he sometimes did?

There was nothing. The movie sign, opposite, was off. The second show had finished more than half an hour ago and the last cars had gone. On his way back from Musak's house Dave Galloway had not met a soul.

Only twice before had Ben returned home after midnight without having warned his father. On both occasions he had waited up for Ben, seated in his armchair, unable to read or listen to the radio. Only when he heard the boy's footsteps on the stairs had he hastily picked up a magazine.

"I'm sorry I'm late."

He spoke lightly, to make the thing seem unimportant. Had he expected a scolding, a scene?

Dave had simply said:

"I was worried."

"About what could have happened to me? I was in Chris Gillespie's car and we had a breakdown."

"Why didn't you telephone?"

"There were no houses there and we had to fix it ourselves."

That time it was at the beginning of winter. The second time, between Christmas and New Year's, Ben had come upstairs more loudly than usual and, once in the room, had deliberately turned away his head, avoided coming near his father.

". . . I'm sorry. . . . I was held up by a friend. . . . Why didn't you go to bed? . . . What are you worried about?"

It was not his voice. For the first time there was something changed in him, almost aggressive. His attitude, his gestures were those of a stranger. Galloway, however, had pretended to notice nothing. On the Sunday morning Ben had slept late, a restless slumber, and when he had appeared in the kitchen his face had been ashen.

His father had allowed him time to have his breakfast, trying to appear as casual as possible, and only at the end had murmured:

"You were drinking, weren't you?"

It had never happened before. Dave lived in sufficiently close intimacy with his son to be sure that until then he had never touched a glass of liquor.

"Don't be mad at me, Dad."

And, after a silence, in a low voice:

"Don't be afraid. I don't want to do it again. I wanted to do the same as the others. I hate it."

"Sure?"

Ben had smiled as he repeated, meeting his eyes:

"Sure."

Since then, that is to say, since December, he had not once come home after eleven. Generally, when Galloway returned from his visit to Musak, he found him sitting in front of the television set, watching the fight, the one whose echoes had just now reached him as he walked down the street. They sometimes watched the finish of it side by side.

"Aren't you hungry?"

Galloway would go into the kitchen, make sandwiches, return with two glasses of cold milk.

With the window open, so as to hear Ben's footsteps at a greater distance, he sat down in the same place as on the two previous occasions when he had awaited him. The air from outside was cold, but he didn't get up to shut the window. He thought for a moment of putting on his coat, told himself that if Ben found him seated like that in his armchair he would have a shock.

The first time he had come home at midnight, the second time at about one in the morning.

He lit a cigarette, then another and yet another, smoking them nervously without being conscious of doing so. At one moment he went and turned on the television, but no picture appeared on the luminous screen. All the programs one could get in Everton were ended.

He did not walk up and down, despite his interior tension, stayed motionless, his eyes fixed on the door until they became cold with the strain, without any precise idea in his head. More than three quarters of an hour had passed when he got up, calm in appearance, and again went toward his son's room.

He did not turn on the light, did not think of it, so that the room, lighted only by the glow from the room next door, was a little ghostly, the bed in particular, of a dull white that evoked tragic images.

One would have said that Galloway knew what he had come in search of, what he was going to find. A pair of dirty shoes lay crosswise on the rug, and a shirt had been thrown over the back of a chair.

At some time during the evening Ben had come in to change his clothes. His everyday suit lay on the floor in a corner of the room, his socks a little farther off.

Slowly Dave opened the wardrobe, and what struck him instantly was the absence of the suitcase. Its place was on the floor, below the clothes hung on hangers. It was two years since Galloway had bought it for his son, on the occasion of a trip they had taken together to Cape Cod, and since then it had not been used.

It had still been there that morning, he was sure of it, because it was he who tidied up the apartment every day. The cleaning woman came only twice a week, for a few hours, on Tuesday and Friday, to do the heavy cleaning.

Ben had come back to put on his best suit and had gone off, taking his suitcase with him. He had not left any message.

Curiously, there was no surprise in Galloway's eyes, as though for a long time, always, he had lived in the expectation of a catastrophe.

Perhaps, however, he had never envisaged this particular catastrophe. With slow movements, even slower than usual, like a man struggling to postpone disaster, he thrust open the door of the bathroom, which served them both, and turned on the light.

On the glass shelf there was now only one razor. The electric razor he had bought Ben for his last Christmas had disappeared. His comb was not there either, nor the toothbrush in its holder. He had even taken the tube of toothpaste.

Because of the bathroom ventilator, still open, a draft blew through the apartment, stirred the curtains, caused the pages of a newspaper lying on the television to flutter.

He returned to the living room to shut the window, stood for a moment staring out, his forehead pressed to the cold glass pane.

He felt as exhausted as after a walk of several hours and there was no more strength in his limbs. He was tempted to go and lie flat on his stomach on his bed and talk by himself, talk to Ben, with his head in the pillow. But what good would that do?

There remained one thing for him to know and he was going to find it out immediately. He did not hurry. He had no reason to hurry. He even took the time to put on his light overcoat and a cap, because he felt frozen.

The moon had risen, almost full, brilliant, and the sky resembled a bottomless sea. On that side of the building garages occupied all the ground floor and he went toward his own, pulled a bunch of keys out of his pocket, thrust one into the lock.

He had no need to turn the key. The door moved at once and a split in the wood showed that it had been forced with a screw driver and another tool.

What need was there to make sure that the garage was empty? It was; the car was no longer there. He knew it already. He had realized it instantly, upstairs. He did not turn on the light. It was not worth the trouble.

He closed the door, nevertheless, with as much care as usual. What was he doing, standing, alone, in a sort of courtyard that lay behind the building, where only one window, his own, was lighted?

He had no reason to remain out of doors. He had nothing to do there.

But henceforth what had he to do at home?

He went upstairs again, however, treading slowly, as though at every stair he paused to reflect, locked the door once more, took off his coat, his cap, which he put back in their place, and went toward his armchair.

Then, his body limp, he stared at the blankness around him.

2

It happens that in dreams we find ourselves suddenly transported to the border of a countryside at once strange and familiar, agonizing as a precipice. Nothing in it resembles what we have known in real life and yet we feel something stir in our memory, we have the near certainty of having been that way before, perhaps of having lived there in a previous dream or in a former life.

Dave Galloway, too, had already lived once before the hour he was now in the act of living, with the same sense of total collapse in his body and in his spirit and the same emptiness around him; on that previous occasion, too, he had lain limply in the green armchair, opposite the matching sofa, which they had originally bought on credit, his wife and he, in a furniture store in Hartford, together with the two low tables, the two chairs and the radio console, because television did not yet exist.

The room, there, was smaller; the house, like all the others on the block, was new; they had been the first to live in it and the trees were only just beginning to come to life on the two sides of the newly made road.

It was at Waterbury, Connecticut. At that time he was working in a factory making watches and precision instruments. He recalled details of that evening as minutely as, no doubt, he would later recall the evening he had just spent with Musak. He had gone to the house of a friend, who worked in another department, to repair a pendulum clock dating from the time of his great-grandfather.

The clock, of German origin, had a finely engraved pewter

face and the movement had been made by hand. Dave had stood on a chair in his shirt sleeves, his head almost touching the ceiling, and he remembered moving the hands to regulate the striking of the hours, the half hours, and the quarters. The windows were open. Then, too, it had been in the spring, a little earlier in the season, and a big bowl of strawberries had stood on the table beside the rye and the glasses. His friend's wife was named Patricia. She was dark-haired, of Italian origin, with a skin of very fine texture. In order to be with them she had brought her ironing board into the living room, and all the time he had been there she had ironed diapers, except when one of the children had awakened and she had gone to soothe it back to sleep. She had three, aged four years, two and a half, and one year, and she was pregnant again, calm and glowing as a ripe fruit.

"Good luck!"

"And yours!"

On that occasion also he had had two ryes. His friend had wanted to pour himself a third, but Patricia had gently called him on it.

"Aren't you afraid of having a headache in the morning?"

They were delighted at hearing the striking of the clock, which had not chimed since they had inherited it. Galloway had been happy too at having spent the evening with them and handled a beautiful piece of mechanism. He remembered that they had tried to calculate what a clock like that would cost if it were made in these days.

"A nightcap?"

Like Musak!

"No, thanks."

He had walked home. He lived only two blocks away. The moon was bright. From the corner Galloway had noticed that there was no light in his house. Ruth must have gone to bed without waiting for him. This was curious because, at night, she never wanted to go to bed and found all sorts of pretexts for delay. He had perhaps been wrong to stay so long?

He quickened his pace, accompanied by the sound of his soles on the cement of the alley. Twenty yards from his house he was already searching in his pocket for the key. And, with the door open, he had instantly had the same impression of emptiness he had had that evening on entering his apartment. He had not even turned on the light. The moon shed enough light in the rooms through the uncurtained windows. He went toward the bedroom, a name on his lips:

"Ruth!"

The bed was undisturbed. There was no one there. An old pair of shoes lay on the rug. Then he had opened the other door and stood motionless, trembling with the fear he had suddenly felt. Ruth had not taken the baby! Ben was there, in his cradle, quite warm, peaceful, spreading a good odor of fresh bread.

"Don't you think he smells of warm bread?" he had once said to his wife.

She had answered, without unkindness, he was sure, simply because it was her way of thinking:

"He smells of wet, like all babies."

He had not picked him out of his crib to clasp him in his arms as he wanted to do. He had only bent down to listen to his breathing for a long time, then, on tiptoe, had returned to their bedroom, where he had turned on the light.

She had not shut the wardrobe and a drawer of the dressing table was pulled out wide, with two black hairpins in it. The room was still impregnated with the strong, vulgar scent she affected, which she must have used at the moment of leaving.

She had taken all her things with her, except a flowered cotton housecoat and two torn pairs of panties.

He had not wept or clenched his fists. He had gone and sat down in the armchair in the living room, near the radio. Long afterward he had gone into the kitchen to make sure she had not left a note for him on the table. There was none. Nevertheless he had not been entirely mistaken. In the garbage pail, by the sink, he found a number of scraps of paper, which he had sufficient patience to fit together like the pieces of a puzzle.

She had meant to leave him a message, but had not managed to write one. She had started several, in her scrawling hand, with spelling mistakes.

"My dear Dave . . ."

She had crossed out "dear" and substituted "poor" and on that sheet there was nothing more except the beginning of a sentence:

"When you read this . . ."

She had torn it up. She had written on the scratch pad hanging in the kitchen, which was used for noting orders to be given to the grocer, who called every morning. She must have sat at the same table where, every day, she sat down to peel vegetables.

"My dear Dave,
I know I'm going to hurt you, but I can't stand it any longer and it's better for it to happen now than later. I've often wanted to talk to you about it, but . . ."

Incapable, no doubt, of expressing exactly what she had in mind, she had torn this one up as well. The third had no form of address.

"We aren't right for one another, I knew it from the start. It has all been a mistake. I'm leaving you the baby. Good luck."

"Good luck" had been crossed out, replaced by: *"Be happy, both of you."*

At the last minute she had changed her mind again, because this note had been torn up like the others, thrown in the pail. She had preferred to leave without saying anything. What was the use? What could words have added? Wasn't it better for him to think what he chose?

He had gone back again to his armchair, convinced that he would not sleep that night, and Ben's crying had awakened him at six in the morning when the house was already bathed in sunshine. It was always he, morning and evening, who gave him his bottle. After a few weeks cereals were added, and vegetable purée during the last days. He knew how to put on diapers, as well. It was the first thing he had wanted to learn when Ruth and the baby had come out of the hospital.

That was fifteen and a half years ago and he had never seen Ruth again; the only time he had had indirect news of her had been when, three years later, he had received a visit from a lawyer who had got him to sign papers in order that his wife might obtain a divorce.

He was not asleep. His eyes remained wide open, staring at the sofa, which had followed him with the rest of his household when he had left Waterbury.

It was he who had brought up Ben, by himself, because he entrusted him only to a woman neighbor, who had four children, during his working hours. All his free time, all his nights, he had passed with his son and he had not once gone out in the evening, had not put his foot inside a movie.

The war had prevented him from leaving the house in Waterbury when he had intended, because his job was frozen in the factory, which converted to defense work. Only later had he looked around for a place where he could start on his own so as not to be obliged to leave the house. It was on purpose, for Ben's sake, that he had chosen a town where existence was peaceful.

Suddenly he had a wild hope. Footsteps had sounded behind the building where no one had any reason to be at that time, and for an instant the thought had crossed his mind that it was his son returning. He forgot that Ben had gone off with the car, and that he would first have heard the engine, the brakes, the slam of the door.

The footsteps drew nearer, not those of one person, but of two, and their rhythm was strange; one felt in it a sort of stumbling. Someone down below put a foot on the first step of the stairway at the same time as the murmur of a woman's voice was audible. Heavy soles that seemed to hesitate came down on the second step, on the third. He went and opened the door, turned on the light, and asked:

"What is it?"

He did not understand, stood there, astounded, above the staircase, watching Bill Hawkins, who, completely drunk, his mustache damp, his hat filthy, looked him up and down besottedly.

Isabel Hawkins, in indoor clothes, in her apron, without hat or coat, as though she had had to leave her house in a great hurry, was trying to squeeze in front of her husband.

"Don't take any notice of him, Mr. Galloway. He's in his usual state again."

He knew them just as he knew all the people in Everton. Hawkins worked as a hand on a neighboring farm and about three nights a week got so drunk that he sometimes had to be brought in from the street, where he might have been run over by a car.

One saw him pass, with a lurching gait, muttering indistinctly into his reddish mustache, which was beginning to turn a dirty white.

They lived near the railway tracks, a little out of town; they must have had eight or nine children; the two eldest, married, lived at Poughkeepsie, one daughter, at least, went to high school, and the ones best known were two twin boys about twelve years old, red-haired and shaggy, wild in appearance, who were the terror of the village.

Hawkins, incapable of coming any higher, his body swaying, his two hands clinging to the stair rail, tried to speak and could not find words. All the way there his wife must have been trying to persuade him to come home. She must have said to him:

"Stay here if you want to. I'll go on home. . . ."

Despite the size of her family she found time to go out as a domestic help and for some months had been working at the Old Barn.

"I'm sorry to disturb you at this hour, Mr. Galloway. Bill, let me pass. Just lean against the wall."

The man fell down and she struggled to get him on his feet again while Galloway, at the top of the stairs, did not move. There was in this scene, lighted by a single yellowish light bulb, something grotesque and a little unreal.

"I suppose your son hasn't come home?"

He did not understand. Incapable of grasping any connection between these people and Ben's leaving.

"Wait while I get by so I don't have to yell. People are sleeping."

There were a few. Most of the people in the shops on the ground floor lived in the residential quarter. It was an old woman, a Pole, who lived next door to Galloway; she had witnessed the massacre, lasting a few minutes, of her husband, her three children, her son-in-law, and her granddaughter, a few months old. She still did not understand why she had been spared, scarcely spoke any English, lived by doing small dressmaking jobs, mending, because she would not have been able to cut out a dress. Her hair entirely white, her face almost without wrinkles, she looked attentively at the people who spoke to her and, understanding only an occasional word, she smiled at them gently, as though to apologize. A married couple lived at the end of the hall, people whose children were married and in New York; the husband worked as a mechanic in the garage across the way. Had the Hawkinses awakened them?

Bill Hawkins was still trying to show his indignation, and not succeeding except with grunts. His wife reached the top of the stairs.

"I had to come out just as I was, to run after him, because I didn't want him to come alone to see you. Do you know what's happened?"

He could not invite her in because of the drunken man still on the stairs, and they remained standing on the landing in front of the half-open door.

Isabel Hawkins saw that he did not understand her. She was not angry.

"What do you mean?" he asked.

"About Ben and my daughter. They've run away."

She had tears in her eyes, but one felt that they were mechanical, conventional tears, that in reality she was not affected by any violent grief.

"I knew he'd taken a fancy to her. He used to hang around the house every night, and more than once I've caught them hanging on to each other in the dark. I didn't pay much attention. I didn't think it was serious. But you, you didn't know?"

"No."

She exclaimed, gazing at him:

"Ah!"

Then she was silent for a moment, as though this had upset her ideas.

"He didn't tell you he was going away?"

"He didn't tell me anything."

"When did you find out?"

"Just now, when I came home."

It was painful to him to have to account for Ben to this woman he hardly knew.

"He took the car," she said, as though she knew it already.

"Yes."

"I heard the engine somewhere near the house."

"What time?"

"Maybe ten. I didn't look at the clock."

"Did you think it was he?"

"No. I just heard a car starting up. I was busy in the front room, mending the children's shirts. The car was on the street in back."

"Your daughter was out of doors?"

"I suppose so. At home, you never know, because everyone comes and goes in the house, goes in and out without anyone bothering."

Her husband, down below, made a wide gesture with his arm, as though telling her to be quiet, shouted a word that must have been:

"Bastard!"

"Be quiet, Bill. It isn't Mr. Galloway's fault, and I'm sure he's just as worried as we are. Aren't you, Mr. Galloway?"

He said yes, reluctantly, asked in his turn:

"You're sure your daughter's with him?"

"Who else would she go with? It's more than two months now that they've been going together, and she hasn't seen any other boys; she hasn't even been seeing her girl friends. She never had a boy friend before him, and I was almost worried about it, because she wasn't like other girls her age."

"What made you sure she'd gone?"

"It was after half-past eleven when Steve, who's seventeen— he's at high school too—came home from the show, and I asked him if his sister was with him. He said he hadn't seen her. At first I thought your son must have brought her back and they were still hidden somewhere in the dark. I opened the door. I called:

" 'Lillian! Lillian!'

"Then I stopped calling, for fear of waking the children. When I came in again Steve said:

" 'She isn't in her room.'

"He had been to look.

" 'You're sure she wasn't at the movies?'

" 'I'm sure.'

" 'You didn't see Ben either?'

"They're friends, Ben and Steve. That's how things started with Lillian. The boys were always going out together and your son often came and had a sandwich with us.

"I could see Steve was starting to think. He's the most serious of them all and he gets the best marks at school.

" 'Did Ben come tonight?' he asked me.

" 'I didn't see him.'

"And then he rushed up to his sister's room for the second time. I heard him pulling out the drawers. He came back and said:

" 'She's gone.' "

The voice was not dramatic. The tone was as monotonous as a lament. Now and then she wrinkled her forehead in her desire to say everything, to forget nothing, and she continued to keep an eye on her husband, who had ended up by sitting on one of the stairs with his back to her, pursuing his silent monologue and wagging his head.

"I went up in my turn to have a look and I found that Lillian had taken her best things with her. When I got back to the kitchen, where Father seemed to be asleep in his armchair, I told Steve about the car I'd heard and Steve said:

" 'I don't understand.'

"I asked him what he didn't understand, seeing Ben had been running after his sister for months.

" 'Because he hasn't any money,' he said.

" 'How do you know?'

" 'Only yesterday some of the boys went to Mack's, and Ben wouldn't go with them because he said he didn't have any money.'

" 'Perhaps it wasn't true.'

" 'I'm sure it was true.'

"They knew each other among themselves better than we do, isn't that so?"

Galloway said:

"Won't you come in?"

"I'd rather not leave him all alone. You know, he wouldn't do anyone any harm. I don't know exactly when he woke up, or what he heard. Every Saturday he's like this. An idea suddenly struck me and I went and looked in the box where we keep the week's money. At half-past six, I'd put in the thirty-eight dollars my husband brought me."

In a noncommittal voice, without inflection, Galloway questioned:

"The money wasn't there?"

"No. She must have done it when I left the kitchen or else when I had my back turned. Don't think I'm blaming anyone. It's not your son I'm accusing. Most likely they don't either of them realize what they're doing."

"What did your son say?"

"Nothing. He had something to eat and went to bed."

"He doesn't like his sister?"

"I don't know. They've never got on very well. It was my husband who suddenly went out, without a word, before I had a chance to stop him, and I ran after him on the street. What are you going to do?"

What could he do?

"Do you think they're going to get married?" she asked him. "Lillian's only fifteen and a half. It's not that she's big, but she looks so serious that people think she's older than she is."

She had come to his shop a few times, like all the girls in the district, to buy knickknacks, a bracelet, a necklace, a ring, a pin. He did not recall her as redheaded, like all the other Hawkinses, but rather as a brunette. He tried to understand, to see her through Ben's eyes. She was thin, slightly round-shouldered, less developed than the other girls of her age. But perhaps this picture of her dated from some months back and she had changed since. He had thought she had a sulky manner, almost sly.

"I read somewhere," Isabel Hawkins went on, "that there are states in the South where they marry them from the age of twelve. Do you think that's where they've gone and they'll write to us afterwards?"

He did not know. He did not know anything. On that other night, fifteen and a half years ago, he had not lost everything, something had remained for him to cling to, a baby in its cradle who, at six in the morning, cried for its bottle.

This time his distress was so great that he was almost tempted to cling to this woman, with her shapeless body, whom he scarcely knew.

"Your daughter never talked to you about her plans?"

"Never. I've an idea that in her heart she was a little ashamed of her family. We're poor people. Her father isn't always presentable and I can understand that it isn't nice, for a young girl . . ."

"How did my son behave when he was with you?"

"He was always very nice, very polite. Once when I was trying to repair a shutter the wind had loosened, he took the hammer out of my hand and did it very well. Whenever he had a glass of milk, he always washed the glass and put it back in its place. But there's no use our talking about all that tonight. It's time I put Bill to bed and you went to bed too. I was only wondering if we should tell the police."

"You have the right to do so if you think you should."

"That isn't what I mean. What I was wondering was whether we're supposed to tell them. The way things are, the police couldn't do anything about it anyway, could they?"

He did not reply. He was thinking of the thirty-eight dollars, of Ben, who, indeed, did not ordinarily have more than three or four dollars in his pocket and never asked for money. Every week his father gave him five dollars and Ben slipped the money into his pocket with an embarrassed air and a thank you.

Dave thought also of the car, which was not in a condition to make a long trip. He had had it over six years and had bought it secondhand. He scarcely used it except when he went to work on other premises. Like his friend at Waterbury, people often asked him to put an antique clock in order. It was he, too, who looked after the Council Office clock, those of the school, the Episcopal and Methodist churches. The back of the car was arranged as a sort of workshop.

Months ago he should have changed the tires. Moreover, after a few miles the engine began to heat up, and if Ben did not remember to refill the radiator frequently it would not do a hundred miles without a serious breakdown.

He was suddenly annoyed with himself for not having bought a new car, for having always postponed that expense.

"I hope they won't get themselves arrested on the road," went on Isabel Hawkins, sighing.

She added as she turned toward the stairs:

"Well! Let's hope everything will turn out all right. You can't do just what you'd like with children and it isn't for our own sakes that we have them. Get up, Hawkins!"

She was strong enough to be able to lift him by one arm and push him in front of her, gently, without his now bothering to make any resistance. Raising her head, she concluded:

"If I hear any news, I'll let you know. But I'd be surprised if my daughter's the first to write!"

He still heard her, outside, murmuring:

"Look where you're going. Hold on to me. Don't drag your feet like that."

The moon had vanished and it would take them half an hour, perhaps an hour, to get home, stopping every ten yards in the darkness of the road.

Ben was on the road too, no doubt with Lillian pressed against him, and he would have his eyes fixed on the luminous track of the headlights. These gave a bad light, the left one especially, which sometimes went out for no reason and then started working again, like some radio receivers, after one gave it a few jolts. Would Ben remember this? If the police stopped him to examine his papers, as happens at night, would they consider his driver's license valid?

It was perhaps deliberately, in order not to think of other things, that he occupied his mind with these minor problems. He was once more alone, in the apartment where only the living room was lighted, and, as fifteen and a half years previously, it did not occur to him to go to bed, or to light a cigarette; he remained seated in his armchair staring straight in front of him.

Legally the driver's license was not valid, at least not in New York State, where the age limit is eighteen years. It was curious that two months ago, in March, Ben should have gone to a little town in Connecticut, thirty miles from Everton, to pass his driving test. He had not told his father, had simply said that he was going out with a friend who had a car. It was not until a week later, one evening when they were alone in the apartment, that he had pulled his wallet out of his pocket, extracted from it a slip of paper.

"What is it?" Dave had asked.

"Look."

"A driver's license? You know that just the same you aren't allowed to use the car in New York State?"

"I know."

"Well?"

"Well, nothing. I passed the test for fun."

He was proud of the scrap of printed paper that bore his name and, in his eyes, made a man of him.

"You could answer all the questions?"

"Easily. I studied the instruction book."

"Where did you say you lived?"

"In Waterbury. They don't ask for proof. I borrowed a car with Connecticut plates from my friend's uncle."

Ben had known how to drive for at least two years, had been familiar with the car for much longer. At the age of ten he was capable of putting it into the garage and taking it out and later he often practiced behind the building.

Dave had returned the license to him with a smile.

"Mind you don't use it!"

According to Isabel Hawkins, at that time he was already meeting Lillian in the evenings. He went to call on her parents as a friend of Steve, ate a sandwich with the others, helped himself to milk, and washed his glass as though he were one of the household.

The most difficult thing to picture was Ben, who in his own home never did anything with his hands, who had never even learned to make a bed properly or to clean his shoes, taking the tools and offering to repair Mrs. Hawkins' shutter.

Dave suddenly realized that he was jealous and that, just now, when the woman had told him her story, it was jealousy that had pumped the blood into his face.

He had never entered the Hawkins house. He had seen it in passing, a big, ramshackle, wooden shanty that had not been repainted for years, with garbage scattered over a patch of wasteland and always, around the porch, children and puppies squealing. For fear of running over one or the other, since they rushed out onto the street when one least expected it, he was always careful to sound his horn.

The twins, with coppery hair, were the boys who were always riding bicycles along the sidewalks without holding the handle bars, uttering Indian yells.

For at least two months, perhaps for three, Ben had seen these people every day and no doubt he had ended by considering himself to some extent one of the family.

In his talks with his father he had divulged none of this. At no moment had he felt any need to confide in him. Young as he was, he already took care not to reveal himself. Dave recalled the first time he had taken him to nursery school, when he was only four years old. He had not cried, had simply given his father a long, reproachful look as the latter went away. When he came to bring him home, Dave had asked anxiously:

"How did you like it?"

Imperturbably, without smiling, the child had answered:

"All right."

"Is the teacher nice?"

"I think so."

"And the other children?"

"Yes."

"What did you do?"

"Play."

"Nothing else?"

"No."

Day after day, during the following months, Dave had asked similar questions and the answers had always been the same.

"You like it at school?"

"Yes."

"Do you have more fun than at home?"

"I don't know."

Long afterwards, by means of questions and deduction, Dave had discovered that there was a bigger and stronger boy in the class who had made Ben his special victim.

"Does he hit you?"

"Sometimes."

"What with?"

"With his fists, with anything, or he pushes me to make me fall in the mud."

"You don't defend yourself?"

"I'll beat him when I'm as big as he is."

"The teacher lets him do it?"

"She doesn't see him."

His legs were short in those days, and his head seemed too big for his body. His father often caught him, when he thought he wasn't being watched, gravely murmuring sentences under his breath.

"What are you saying, Ben?"

"Nothing."

"Who are you talking to?"

"To me."

"And what are you telling yourself?"

"Stories."

He did not say what stories. It was his secret domain. For a long time Dave had wondered what answers he would give the child when he asked him questions about his mother. It was repugnant to him, from a feeling akin to superstition, to pretend that she was dead. How explain to him that she had gone away and that he would probably never see her?

But at no age had Ben put the question. He was nearly seven when they had been able to leave Waterbury. Had his little school-fellows, having heard their parents talk about it, told him the truth?

If so, he had betrayed no sign of the fact. He was not a morose boy. He was not repressed, either. Like all children, he had explosions of noisy gaiety.

"You're happy, Ben?" his father often asked him, trying to speak lightly.

"Yes."

"You're sure you're happy?"

"Sure."

"You wouldn't want to change places with any other boy?"

"No."

It was an indirect way of knowing. Once, when Ben was thirteen and they were walking together in the country, Dave had murmured:

"You know I'm your friend, Ben?"

"I know."

"I'd like you always to think of me as your friend, never to be afraid to tell me everything."

Galloway had not dared to say more, because he had a feeling that the boy was embarrassed. Ben had always been very shy of his feelings.

"If, someday, you want to ask me questions, ask them and I promise to answer absolutely frankly."

"What questions?"

"I don't know. Sometimes one wonders why people do this or that, why they live in one way or another."

"I haven't any questions."

And he started to throw stones into a pond.

It was seven in the morning when the telephone rang in the

shop, setting up a vibration that could be felt through the floor. Dave instantly collected himself, wondered if he would have time to go downstairs, walk around the building, and go into the shop before the switchboard operator gave up.

This had sometimes happened. If it was Ben, he knew and would call again in a few minutes.

At the corner of the alleyway Dave could still hear it ringing, but by the time he opened the door it had stopped.

The sun had the same kind of brilliance as the moon during the night. The streets were empty. Birds were hopping on the lawn in front of the Colonial.

His limbs stiff, he stayed there waiting, his eyes fixed on the telephone, while the open door let in the fresh morning air.

One or two cars passed, people from New York or its suburbs on their way to the country. He felt mechanically in his pockets for cigarettes. He must have left them upstairs.

They didn't call back. He did not really believe that it was Ben who had called; he could not have explained why.

A half hour went by. Then another quarter of an hour. He wanted a cigarette, a cup of coffee, but he dared not go upstairs in case he should miss another call.

Ben, who often wanted to call up his friends in the evening, had asked him to have a telephone installed in the apartment. Why had he always put off this expense?

It must have been very late when he had fallen asleep. His slumber had been both heavy and disturbed, so that now he felt more tired than he had the previous evening.

He nearly rang up Musak. To say what to him? To tell him what had happened? They had never talked together about their personal affairs, Dave had never talked about them to anyone.

He stood with his elbows on the counter, his eyelids smarting, and he was still in that posture when a car drove along Main Street at high speed, turned the corner, and pulled up in front of the shop.

Two men in the uniform of the state police got out, both of whom had faces that were fresh and rested, close-shaven. They raised their heads to look at the name over the window and one of them consulted a notebook he had pulled out of his pocket.

Without waiting Galloway went to meet them, well knowing that it was he they were looking for.

3

Standing in the doorway, blinking because of the morning sunlight, which hit him full in the face, he half parted his lips to ask:

"Has my son had an accident?"

He could not have said what stopped him, whether it was his intuition or something in the attitude of the two men. They seemed surprised to find him there, exchanged glances as though questioning one another. Did they wonder about his unshaven face and his clothes creased by the hours he had spent in his armchair?

There was a state-police station at Radley, almost opposite the high school, and Galloway knew, at least by sight, the six men attached to it, two of whom were in the habit of stopping their car outside his shop when the clock needed repairing.

These two were not from Radley. They must have come from Poughkeepsie or farther off.

He would probably have ended by asking his question nonetheless, if only for the sake of form, if the shorter of the two had not said:

"Your name is Dave Clifford Galloway?"

"It is."

After consulting his notebook the patrolman went on:

"You are the owner of a Ford car, license number 3M-2437?"

He nodded. Now he was on the defensive. His instinct warned him that he must protect Ben. He said in a casual voice, as though he did not think it important:

"Has there been an accident?"

They looked oddly at one another before one of them answered:

"No. No accident."

He must not talk any more. From now on he would just answer questions. When they tried to see into the shop over his shoulder, he stepped back to let them enter.

"Are you working at eight o'clock on a Sunday morning?"

It was no doubt intended to be ironical, since the display window was empty and the watches under repair were not hanging on their hooks above the bench.

"I wasn't working. I live on the floor above. About half an hour ago, I heard the telephone ringing through the floor. I came down. I had to walk around the building and when I got here they had hung up. I stayed because I thought they might call again."

"It was we who called up."

From their disconcerted aspect Dave could have sworn they had expected something else. They were not threatening. Embarrassed, rather.

"Did you drive your car last night?"

"No."

"Is it in your garage?"

"It isn't there any more. It disappeared last night."

"When did you find out?"

"Between half-past eleven and midnight, when I came back from the house of a friend where I'd spent the evening."

"Can you give me his name?"

"Frank Musak. He lives on the first street on the right past the post office."

The one with the notebook wrote down the name and address.

Galloway did not lose his calm. He was not afraid. The fact of being questioned in this fashion by patrolmen in uniform nevertheless gave him the feeling of being no longer a citizen quite like others. People occasionally went by outside, in particular young girls, children in Sunday clothes, who were on their way to the Catholic church and cast a curious glance at the open shop and the two patrolmen.

"You found out that your car wasn't in the garage when you got home?"

"That's right."

"You didn't go out again during the night?"

"No."

He was not lying, but he was deceiving them nonetheless, and he was afraid he would start blushing. Once again they exchanged glances, withdrew to a corner of the shop where they talked in undertones; Galloway, mechanically, had gone behind his counter, as when he was receiving a customer, and he did not try to hear what they were saying.

"Will you let me use your telephone? Don't worry: we'll have the call charged to us."

The man called the operator.

"Hullo! State police. Will you give me the Hortonville station? . . . Yes . . . thanks."

The weather was brilliant. The bells began to ring in full strength and the lawn opposite, over which the trees cast long blue shadows, was dotted with yellow flowers.

"That you, Fred? Dan. Let me talk to the lieutenant, will you?"

He had only an instant to wait. He talked in an undertone, almost a whisper, his hand to his mouth.

"We've arrived, Lieutenant. He's here . . . Hello! . . . Yes . . . we found him in his shop. . . . No . . . Seems he wasn't doing anything. . . . He lives on the second floor and heard the phone ring. . . . It's a little hard to explain. . . . The way the place is arranged, he has to leave his apartment and walk around the building, it's pretty long. . . . Yes . . . Yes . . . Seems the car disappeared from the garage last night before half-past eleven. . . ."

The voice of the lieutenant caused the receiver to vibrate, but Galloway could not hear what he was saying. The patrolman, with the receiver in his hand, still seemed rather perplexed.

"Yes. . . . Yes. . . . That's right. . . . There's something strange . . ."

During this time he continued to scrutinize Galloway with a curiosity free from hostility.

"Maybe that would be better, yes. . . . In about an hour . . . a little more. . . ."

He hung up, lit a cigarette.

"The lieutenant would like you to come with me to identify your car."

"Can I go upstairs and shut the doors?"

"If you want to."

Dave slipped the spring lock and they both followed him to the other side of the building. One of the patrolmen at once noticed the fresh split in the garage door.

"Is this yours?"

"Yes."

He pulled open a wing of the door to look inside, where there was nothing but a black oil stain on the concrete floor where the car should have been.

Dave started up the stairs and the shorter of the two patrolmen followed him, as though, again with a sign, they had concerted their actions.

"I suppose I haven't time to make myself a cup of coffee?"

"It'll be faster for us to stop at a restaurant on the way."

The man was gazing about him, still surprised, rather like someone who fears he has come to the wrong door. While Dave was combing his hair and splashing cold water on his face, he looked inside the two bedrooms.

"You don't seem to have been to bed!" he remarked.

Then, as Galloway sought for a reply, he hurried to add:

"It's not my business. You don't have to tell me anything."

A little later, in the same detached voice, he questioned again —and it was more a remark than a question:

"You aren't married?"

Dave wondered what there was about the apartment that caused him to think this. He had always tried, for Ben's sake, to prevent their home seeming like the habitation of men alone. At Musak's place, for example, this had always struck him. No one could mistake it. The very odor revealed that there was no woman in the house.

"I used to be married," he contented himself with replying.

He was behaving like certain sick people who are so afraid of unleashing a crisis that they live in slow motion, with careful movements, only speaking in a lifeless voice.

In his heart he had not been surprised at seeing the patrolmen. Nor had he seriously believed that Ben had had an accident. Besides, if it had been an accident, they would have told him at once. Since he had returned last night to the empty apartment, he had known that it was more serious and he was hunching his shoulders to make himself less vulnerable to fate.

No matter what had happened, he had to protect his son. Never had he felt so sharply, so physically, the bond that existed between them. It was not a separate person who was in trouble somewhere, God knew where—it was a part of himself.

He was bearing himself like an honest man, respectful of the laws, a little apprehensive, but having nothing with which to reproach himself.

"I suppose it doesn't matter that I haven't shaved?"

He was redheaded, not the red of the Hawkins family, a vivid red. His very fine hair was beginning to grow thin and the sun drew glints of gold from his cheeks. Why did he go into the kitchen to make sure that the electric stove was not turned on? From force of habit! He locked his door, downstairs rejoined the second patrolman, to whom his colleague went and spoke a few words.

"Are you coming?"

He had been going to get into the back of the car, but they motioned to him to sit in front and, to his astonishment, only the shorter of the two men got in and took his place at the wheel, while the other remained standing on the sidewalk and watched them go.

"It's always on a Sunday morning that we run into cases of this sort," said his companion in the tone in which he might have chatted to someone in a bar. "On Saturday night, people can't stay quiet!"

It was truly Sunday all along the road. In every town one saw white churches with open doorways, women wearing white gloves and, in one place, little girls walking in line, each with a bouquet in her hand.

"Don't forget my cup of coffee," Dave permitted himself to say with a forced smile.

"We'll come to a good place just past Poughkeepsie."

They went through the city without stopping, crossed the bridge over the Hudson, which sparkled in the sunlight and where at that moment an excursion steamer was passing. . . .

The car entered the first ramparts of the Catskills and the road, twisting, rose and fell, plunged into dark, cool forest, ran alongside a lake, sometimes passed farms and meadows on a plain. In front of a drive-in standing at the edge of the highway, festooned with posters advertising brands of soft drinks, the police officer pulled up, called to a girl in slacks who came toward them:

"Two coffees."

"Black?"

"Black for me," said Dave. "With two lumps of sugar."

"Same for me."

For most people it was a wonderful Sunday. Farther on, they crossed a golf course over which little groups were scattered, their golf bags slung over their shoulders. Nearly all the men were wearing white caps, and a good many of the women were already in shorts, with sunglasses.

Judging by the phone call and the phrases Dave had overheard, it was to Hortonville that he was being taken. He had been there before. It was a town situated near the border between New York State and Pennsylvania. He seemed to remember a police station built of brick, with no upper story, at the edge of the highway. From Everton to Hortonville it was sixty miles, and they took only a little more than an hour and a quarter to cover it.

He was forcing himself to keep silent, to ask no questions, and his hands were damp with the effort, there was sweat on his upper lip.

"You don't smoke?"

"I left my cigarettes behind."

The patrolman offered him his pack, pointed to the electric lighter. They had just passed through a little town still asleep, Liberty, probably, then they had seen a lake of considerable size on which numerous boats appeared motionless. They again entered a forest and Dave suddenly almost stopped his companion, started to lay a hand on his arm.

He had thought he recognized his car at the side of the road, its right-hand wheels in the grass, and he had had time to make out in the shadow the figure of a patrolman.

The movement had not escaped his companion.

"That yours . . . ?" he asked, as though it were of no importance.

"I think . . . yes. . . ."

"We have to see the lieutenant first, about two miles from here, and we'll probably come back afterwards."

The bricks of the police station were of tender pink and there was a flower bed on either side of the door. In contrast with the light outside the interior seemed dark and Galloway felt almost cold, perhaps partly owing to his nervous tension. He even felt, when they left him alone in the passage, a genuine shudder.

"Will you come this way?"

The lieutenant was young, athletic. Dave was surprised when he held out a vigorous hand to him.

"I'm sorry to have caused you this inconvenience, Mr. Galloway, but it was difficult for me to do otherwise."

What had the lieutenant told the patrolman who had brought him, with whom he had had a fairly long talk? The latter was not looking at him now in quite the same way. Dave had the impression that there was a great deal more sympathy in his gaze, indeed a sort of respect.

"You noticed your car on the way here?"

"I thought I recognized it."

"We'd better start with that. It'll only take us a few minutes."

He got down his cap, put it on, and went out to the car, motioning to the other man to come with them.

"It seems you didn't have much luck at backgammon last night?"

They had questioned Musak. They were not attempting to hide the fact. It was as though this were a means of proving that they were dealing with him openly.

"You mustn't be angry with us, Mr. Galloway. You should know that it's our job to check up on everything."

They were already coming within sight of the car and Dave's first glance was at the tires, of which not one was flat; the palms of his hands now were really wet and, as he got out of the car, he wondered for an instant if he were going to be capable of walking.

"You recognize the bus?"

"Certainly."

"Those are watchmaker's tools you have in the back?"

"Yes."

"For a minute I was puzzled, because I couldn't figure out what trade they belonged to. Do you want to take a look inside?"

They opened the door for him and what he instinctively looked at first was the place where Ben had sat. He passed his hand over it, furtively, as though the leather had been able to retain a little of his son's warmth. The white, crumpled object, near the clutch pedal, was a woman's handkerchief smelling of eau de Cologne.

"One of our patrols found the car around two in the morning, but it must have been here some time, because the engine was cold. The headlights had been switched off."

Galloway could not prevent himself from asking:

"Does it run?"

"That's just what intrigued my men. The engine runs, so it wasn't a question of a breakdown."

He called to the man in charge.

"You can drive it to Poughkeepsie," he said.

Dave was on the verge of protesting, of asking why his car wasn't given back to him.

"You coming, Mr. Galloway?"

He was silent while he drove and did not speak a word until they were in his office where the patrolman who had come to Everton followed them.

"Shut the door, Dan."

The lieutenant's manner was grave, embarrassed.

"Cigarette?"

"No, thanks. I didn't have time for any breakfast and . . ."

"I know. You didn't sleep much last night. You didn't even go to bed."

Was Galloway really doing his utmost? Was he doing everything in his power to protect Ben? His fear was that he might not be equal to the occasion. He was not used to trickery.

It seemed to him that the lieutenant read his thoughts on his face. Why did he show him so much consideration when he was only a small-town watchmaker of no importance?

The other man suddenly decided to sit down and ran his hand through his hair, which was stiff, cut short.

"Since you left Everton, Mr. Galloway, we've had news from various sources and it's my duty to tell you about it. We've heard, for instance, that the Hawkinses paid you a visit during the night."

He did not start, did not blink, but it was as though his heart had ceased to beat, because now they must inevitably come to the subject of Ben.

"One of the Hawkins boys, passing on his bicycle, this morning, saw men in uniform in your shop and rushed home to tell his mother. She hurried there right away, hoping they'd be able to give her news of her daughter."

The lieutenant's hands must have been damp as well, because he got his handkerchief out of his pocket and fiddled with it.

"Do you know your son well, Mr. Galloway?"

They had reached it. Dave had hoped that this moment would never come, had tried to hope against all possibility, against all reason. His eyes began to burn, his Adam's apple rose and fell, and the lieutenant turned away his head, out of delicacy, as though to allow him to express his feelings freely.

Was it Dave's voice that answered:

"I think I know him, yes."

"Your son didn't come home last night. The Hawkins girl . . ."

He glanced at his notes, corrected:

". . . Lillian Hawkins left her parents' house during the evening, taking her belongings with her."

He allowed nearly half a minute to pass.

"You knew they had run away together in your car?"

Why deny it? It was he, and not Ben, who was being accused.

"It's what I supposed after the Hawkinses had come."

"It didn't occur to you to notify the police?"

He said frankly:

"No."

"You've never felt any anxiety regarding your son?"

Meeting the lieutenant's eyes, he answered firmly:

"No."

It was not altogether true, but his anxieties had never been of the kind to which the lieutenant was referring. Even an ordinary father could not understand.

"He has never given you any trouble?"

"No. He's a quiet boy, rather studious."

"I've already been told that, last year, he was one of the three best pupils in his class."

"That's true."

"This year, his marks have changed. . . ."

He was about to explain that children are not the same every year, that they grow interested first in one thing, then in another, that in a few years they have to complete a whole cycle. It was the compassion he read in the lieutenant's eyes that prevented him from speaking, and then, very low, his chin on his chest, as though he had given up the contest, he stammered:

"What has he done?"

"Would you like to read the report for yourself?"

He pushed several large-sized sheets of paper across the desk. Dave shook his head. He would have been incapable of reading.

"One mile from here, in the direction of Pennsylvania, but still in New York State, a motorist this morning saw a human form lying at the side of the road. It was half-past five and only just beginning to get light. At first the man drove on, then, conscience-stricken, thinking it might be someone who was injured, he turned back."

The lieutenant was speaking slowly, in a monotonous voice, as one does when reading a report, but he gave only an occasional glance at the papers, which he had again pulled toward him.

"A few minutes later, this man came in here to report that he had found a dead body. I'd just gone on duty at Poughkeepsie when I was notified and I arrived on the spot only a short time after the patrolmen from the station."

Was Dave listening? He could have sworn that the words were no longer words, but pictures passing in front of his eyes like a colored film. He could not have repeated a single one of the phrases uttered, and yet he had the impression of having followed in their comings and goings each one of the persons evoked.

While all this was going on, he had been asleep himself, in his green armchair, facing the window beyond which the sun was rising and the birds were beginning to hop about the lawn.

"From the papers we found in the dead man's pockets, we have established that he was a certain Charles Ralston, of Long Eddy, about twelve miles from here. I called up his home, where his wife told me that last night her husband went to have dinner with their daughter, who's married and lives in the suburbs of Poughkeepsie. His wife has not been well for some weeks, so she couldn't go with him and went to bed early. When she woke up in the middle of the night and found her husband wasn't beside her, she didn't worry, thinking he had decided to spend the night at their daughter's house, which was what he sometimes did, particularly when he had had a drop too much. Charles Ralston was the regional representative of a well-known brand of refrigerator and was fifty-four years old."

He made a pause, let fall:

"He had been killed by a bullet in the nape of the neck, fired at point-blank range, probably when he was seated at the wheel of his car. Then he was dragged to the side of the road, as the surface indications show, and his wallet was searched, the money it contained was taken. According to his wife, he probably had twelve or fourteen dollars on him."

There was a heavy silence, such as prevails sometimes in a court of law when the judgment is read. The first to make any movement was Galloway, and it was to uncross his legs, which were hurting him.

"I can go on?" asked the lieutenant.

He nodded. It was better to get it over.

"The bullet, a 38-caliber, was fired from an automatic. When he left his daughter and his son-in-law, Ralston was driving a blue Oldsmobile sedan, with New York State license plates."

He glanced at his wrist watch.

"It is three hours, now, since the description of this car was sent out by radio in all directions, especially to Pennsylvania, where the car seemed to be heading. A short time before your arrival, the police at Gagleton called up to tell me that last night, about two o'clock, the occupants of a car answering to that description had stopped at a gas station, way out in the country, and had gotten the owner out of bed to fill their tank."

Dave's mouth was dry, burning, and he was unable to swallow; his Adam's apple, stuck, gave him a sense of strangulation.

"The blue Oldsmobile was driven by a young man of medium height, light-complexioned, wearing a light-colored raincoat. A very young girl, who was inside the car, pulled down the window to ask for cigarettes. So as not to have to open up the office, where there was an automatic machine, the garage proprietor gave her his own partly used pack. The young man paid with a ten-dollar bill of which we shall soon have the number."

That was all. What more could one say? The lieutenant waited, without looking at Galloway, finally got up, and gestured to the patrolman to follow him outside. Dave did not move, took no account of the time that passed, and, twice, caught himself dreaming that he was taking a little boy to school. They were merely pictures that passed very quickly over his mind's eye. He was not thinking. The telephone rang and he paid no attention. He could, if he had listened, have heard what was being said over an extension in the other office.

He had not wept. It was certain, now, that he would not weep, that he had passed the point of tears.

When, much later, he raised his eyes, he was surprised to find himself alone; it troubled him and he nearly called out, not daring, of his own accord, to leave the room.

Perhaps they were keeping an eye on him, had heard him move? The lieutenant, in any event, appeared in the doorway.

"I guess you'd like to go home."

He nodded, astonished that they did not keep him prisoner. He would not have protested. It would have seemed to him natural.

"I have to ask you to sign this statement. You can read it. It's simply a declaration by which you formally identify your car."

Didn't this constitute a betrayal of Ben?

"Do I really have to sign?"

The other lowered his eyelids, and Galloway signed submissively.

"I may tell you, between ourselves, that they've gone a long way since last night and that they're already out of Pennsylvania. The last place where they were reported is in western Virginia."

Wouldn't Ben, who'd been driving like this since last night, have to stop and get some sleep?

"They aren't traveling on the highways, they're turning off along lanes and secondary roads, which makes it more difficult to catch up with them."

Galloway was standing and the lieutenant laid a hand on his shoulder.

"If I were in your place—and I'm speaking as a man, not as a police officer—I'd make sure, right away, of getting a good lawyer for your son. He has the right, as you know, not to say anything except in a lawyer's presence, and that sometimes makes all the difference."

"He" meant Ben, incredible though it seemed, Ben, of whom they were suddenly talking as a grown man responsible for his actions. He nearly protested, so monstrous did this seem to him. He was tempted to cry:

"But he's only a child!"

He had given him his bottle. At four years old Ben had still wet his bed, and in the morning was all upset about it. It had mortified him for more than a year.

How many weeks had passed since the last time his father had asked him:

"Happy, Ben?"

He had answered without hesitating, in a voice that, during the past two years only, had grown curiously grave:

"Yes, Dad."

He did not use high-flown phrases. He did not easily unbosom himself. But surely Dave, who had spent sixteen years of his life watching him, must know him better than anyone?

"Will you drive Mr. Galloway home?"

"Shall I bring Dan back?"

"No. He's had instructions by phone."

A broad, muscular hand was again held out, used a little more pressure than the first time.

"Good-by, Mr. Galloway. If this case doesn't pass out of my responsibility, as it may do, I'll keep you informed."

He added after glancing at his desk:

"I have your phone number? . . . Yes. . . ."

Dave had to close his eyes entirely, so dazzling did he find the sunshine, and the air trembled about him; flies buzzed among the flowers in the beds. He found himself seated again in the car, where a voice was saying:

"Maybe I'd better open all the windows."

An arm stretched in front of him to turn the handle and he started.

"Sorry! Come to think of it, you'd have been glad of another cup of coffee, wouldn't you? There was some at the station and I didn't think of offering you any."

He answered mechanically:

"It doesn't matter."

"The lieutenant's a nice man. He has three children. The youngest was born just a week ago, when he was on duty like to-day."

The patrolman reached out, turned a knob, and, after a sound of crackling, they began to hear a nasal voice repeating a figure, the license number of a car. It was only when his companion hastily switched it off, as though without thinking he had been guilty of tactlessness, that Galloway realized that it was the blue Oldsmobile.

The man in uniform made two or three further attempts at conversation, observing the watchmaker from the corner of his eye, and finally resigned himself to silence. The same woods, the same golf course, the same towns swept past, with more cars on the road and parked outside the roadhouses. Ben had passed that way a few hours earlier, with Lillian clinging to him. Would it serve any purpose, at this moment, if Dave cried with all his strength, as though a human voice could be heard across all the states of America, as though distance did not exist:

"Ben!"

He so longed to do it that he clenched his teeth and drove his fingernails into the flesh of his hands. He did not even recognize Poughkeepsie, did not notice when they passed through a town and its suburbs.

And when the car passed the signboard announcing the approach to his own town, he had no sense of returning home, looked at the Old Barn, the First National Store; finally the lawn, the shops, his own shop, that of Mrs. Pinch, that of the hairdresser, as though it were all no more than the empty shell of what had once been his town.

He did not know what time it was. He had lost all sense of time. Time had ceased to exist, like space. How could he believe, for instance, that Ben was now driving over the roads of Virginia, perhaps even over those of Ohio or Kentucky?

Dave had never been to Kentucky and Ben was only a child. Dozens, hundreds of men in the prime of life, trained for that kind of hunt, with perfected equipment, were nevertheless in pursuit of him or trying to track him down.

It was not possible. Nor that in the evening and tomorrow newspapers in America would publish his photograph on the front page as that of a dangerous criminal.

"Shall I drop you behind the building?"

There was never anyone on the sidewalks, on Sundays, during the middle of the day. Directly after church service the streets emptied, became more echoing, and life did not return to them until later for the baseball game.

The policeman went around to the other side of the car to open the door for him, and it was Galloway who held out his hand and said politely:

"Thank you very much."

A strip of adhesive tape, with a wax seal at either end, barred the door of the garage, and sticky paper had been put over the split to protect it. He went upstairs without meeting anyone and he seemed still to see old Hawkins huddled on the steps, talking to himself and wagging his head.

Perhaps at that moment everything had been done. It was almost certain. He did not want to think about it too precisely. And, on the landing, Isabel Hawkins had been talking to him about her daughter and the thirty-eight dollars that had disappeared from the box in the kitchen.

He heard footsteps behind the door of the old Polish lady, who went about all day in slippers because of her swollen legs. They always made a furtive sound, a curious slithering, like that of an invisible animal in the forest.

He opened his door and it was the time when the sun lighted a third of the living room, including a corner of the green sofa. Ben had a habit of stretching out on it, in the evenings, and holding a book above his face.

"You find that position comfortable?"

He'd answer:

"I'm all right."

Galloway did not know what to do with himself. He had not taken off his hat. He no longer thought of making himself coffee, or of eating. He was waiting, at any moment, for the burst of shouting that would indicate the beginning of the baseball game. Through the bathroom ventilator, if you stood on a stool, you could see part of the ground.

What had he come to do in the kitchen? Nothing. He had nothing to do here. He went back into the living room, saw his cigarettes on the radio, didn't touch them. He had no desire to smoke. His knees were trembling agonizingly, but he did not sit down.

The window was closed. It was hot. When he started to sponge his face, he found that he still had his hat on and he took it off.

Then, suddenly, as though this were what he had come to the apartment to do, he went into Ben's room and stretched himself

out full length, face down, on his son's bed, his two hands grip-
ping the pillow, and moved no more.

4

At the beginning he did not do it deliberately, was aware of nothing. If he stayed motionless, it was from lassitude, because he
hadn't the strength to move, or any reason for doing so. Little by
little a heaviness somewhat resembling that of fever took possession of his limbs, of his whole body, and it seemed to him that his
mind, in yielding to it, acquired a more intense life, but on a different plane. It was rather as though—he would not have said it
to anyone, for fear of being laughed at—he gained access to a
higher reality, where all things took on a sharper significance.

This had often happened to him when he was a child. He remembered one time in particular, when he was five years old, in
Virginia. It had perhaps lasted an hour, perhaps only a few minutes, because it was a state like that of dreams, which give the impression of lasting a long time, precisely because time is abolished.
It was in any case his most vivid memory, sufficing in itself to sum
up all his childhood.

He had been lying down then, too, not on his stomach that time,
as he was at present on Ben's bed, but in the open air, on his back,
his hands clasped behind his head, and, with his face turned to the
sun, he had kept his eyes closed while red and golden gleams
pierced his eyelids.

At that period he was losing his first teeth and, in a half-wakeful
state, he worried with the tip of his tongue a tooth that was loose.
It didn't hurt. On the contrary, he derived from it a sensation so
exquisite, spreading in waves, like a fluid, through his being, that
he couldn't believe it was not a sin and afterwards was always ashamed of it.

Never, since then, had he so acutely felt the mingling of his
own life and that of the universe, his heart beating with the same
rhythm as the earth, as the grass that surrounded him, as the leaves

of the trees that rustled above his head. His pulse became the pulse of the world and he was conscious of everything, of the movements of the grasshoppers, of the coolness of the earth that he felt against his back and of the rays of the sun that were scorching his skin; sounds as well, ordinarily confused, detached themselves from one another with a marvelous clarity, the clucking of the hens in the yard, the drone of the tractor on the hillside, the voices on the porch, that of his father above all, who, while he drank his glass of bourbon in little sips, was giving instructions to the colored overseer.

He couldn't see him then, and yet he was sure that the picture he retained of him was as he was on that day, in the violet shadow, with his russet mustache, which he wiped with his forefinger after each sip.

The syllables came to him very distinctly and he had not tried to grasp their sense, because what the words meant was of no importance, what mattered was that his father's voice rose, calm and reassuring, with the other sounds of the earth to lend it a sort of accompaniment.

Sometimes the colored man punctuated a sentence with a "Yes, sir."

And his voice too was different from those he had heard since, coming from the depths of his chest, heavy and pulpy as the flesh of a ripe fruit.

"Yes, sir."

The Southern accent greatly prolonged the "sir," from which the final *r* disappeared, and it became an incantation.

It was in the house where his father had been born. The earth was dark red, the trees of a greener green than anywhere else, and the summer sun had the color and consistency of honey.

Was it not on that occasion that he had vowed to himself to be like his father? When his mother, with the car, drove him to school in the neighboring small town and someone exclaimed that he took after her, he spent the next few days looking in the glass and feeling unhappy.

In the town, too, the dust was red, the wooden houses painted the same syrupy yellow as Musak's house. Perhaps Musak had lived in Virginia?

Everton was arousing itself from its midday torpor, he knew it.

He knew where he was, forgot nothing. But he was capable, without becoming confused, of mingling past and present, of making them one whole, because, finally, they were probably nothing but one whole.

Someone spoke down below, a woman's voice:

"Do you think he's at home?"

When her husband replied, Dave recognized his voice. It was the post office clerk, the man who headed the Fourth of July procession carrying the flag. He murmured, no doubt tugging his wife's arm:

"It seems they brought him back a little while ago. Come on."

Although they spoke in an undertone, he heard everything.

"Poor man!"

They were on their way to the baseball field. Other people passed by. Footsteps scuffled over the dusty stones of the sidewalks, growing more and more numerous. Not everyone stopped, but each one probably raised his head to glance at his windows.

They knew. Through the radio, of course. Early that morning the call had been sent out on the police wave length, then they had decided to make the news known to the public in the ordinary daytime news bulletins.

He had a small radio near him, on the night table; he had no need to look to know that it was there. It was Ben's radio, which he had given him for his twelfth birthday, during the period when he listened every evening, his gaze intent, to a cowboy program.

Was it not strange that Ben, at this moment, might be in that same Virginia of which Dave had so often talked to him but where Ben had never before set foot?

"Is the soil really red?" he had still been asking only a few years ago, incredulously.

"Not red like blood. But it's red. I don't know any other word."

Had they been able to stop for a bite to eat at a drive-in or to buy sandwiches someplace along the road?

Someone passing, a child probably, gave two or three little knocks on his shopwindow. Then, like a theater orchestra, cries burst out on the sports field, there were blasts of the whistle, the usual Sunday tumult, with the spectators getting up on the benches and waving their arms.

One day, not very long after that midday in the grass and the sunshine, it wasn't his mother who came to bring him from school, but one of the colored men on the farm, and when he got home Dave hadn't seen his parents, but had found the maids in tears, gazing compassionately at him.

He had never seen his father again. He had died, about one o'clock, alone in the waiting room of a bank in Culpeper, where he had gone to try to obtain a new loan. His mother had been told by telephone and the body had been taken straight to the undertaker's.

His father had been forty. It was then that the conviction had been implanted in him that, since he resembled him, he too would die at forty. The idea had gained so strong a hold that even now, at the age of forty-three, he was sometimes astonished to find himself alive.

Had Ben, too, ever imagined that he resembled him, that their lives would follow a similar pattern? He had never dared to ask him. He hesitated to put direct questions to him, observed him covertly, tried to guess.

Had his own father had these curiosities, these fears where he was concerned? Was it the same with all fathers and all sons? Very often he had behaved in a particular way only because of the memory of his father and, when he was seventeen, he had let his mustache grow for several months in order to be more like him.

Perhaps, if he had retained so heightened a memory of him, this was connected with the fact that his mother had remarried two years later. He was not sure. The thought often occurred to him, precisely because of Ben, when he had feelings of uneasiness on his account.

Scarcely two weeks after the funeral they had sold the farm in Virginia and had gone to live in a town of which the memory was hateful to him, Newark, New Jersey. He had never known why his mother had chosen that particular town.

"We were ruined," she had told him later, without convincing him. "I had to earn my living and I couldn't go out to work in a place where everyone knows my family."

She was a Truesdell and one of her ancestors had played a part in the Confederacy. But the family of Galloway, which had included a governor and a historian, was no less well known.

At Newark they had no servants, lived on the third floor of a house of dark brick, with an iron outside staircase, in case of fire, which passed in front of their window and stopped on the level of the second floor.

His mother worked in an office. Often she went out in the evenings and a young girl she paid came to look after Dave.

"If you're good, we'll soon go and live in the country again, in a big house."

"In Virginia?"

"No. Not far from New York."

She meant White Plains, where, sure enough, they went to live when she married Musselman.

If he turned on the radio, would he hear something about Ben? Two or three times he had been tempted to do so, but had not had the courage to wrench himself out of his stupor, to return suddenly to naked reality. And if he made the slightest movement, he knew that this would happen, that he would get up, begin to walk about, go and open the window, because it was beginning to grow warm in the apartment. No doubt he would even eat something. He felt gnawing pains in his breast.

Later there would be time. As long as he was in his present state, like the little boy in Virginia, it seemed to him that he was closer to Ben.

Perhaps his son had no desire to be like him? Once when he had been playing with other children on the sidewalk, outside the shop, he had heard one of them, the garageman's son, proclaim:

"My father's stronger than yours. He could knock him down with one punch."

It was true. The garageman was a colossus and Dave had never gone in for sports. He had remained in suspense, waiting for Ben's reaction, and Ben had said nothing.

This had hurt him. It was ridiculous. It hadn't meant a thing. Nevertheless he had felt a twinge at his heart and, after seven years, still remembered it.

What troubled him most of all was when his son, thinking himself unobserved, silently looked at him. At those moments his face was grave, thoughtful. He seemed very far away. Was he making a picture of him such as Dave had made of his own father?

He would have liked to know that picture, to ask: "You aren't too ashamed of me?"

Those words had often trembled on his lips and it was then that he would say, approaching the matter indirectly:

"Are you happy?"

His mother had never put that question to him. Would he have had the courage, if she had done so, to answer: "No!"?

Because he had not been. The mere sight of Musselman, who was a quite important man in the insurance business and felt the need to prove it to himself all day long, was enough to make the house at White Plains intolerable to him. It was because of Musselman, because of his mother, that when he left high school he had gone to a school of watchmaking in order to be able to earn his living soon and not live with them any more. . . .

Last night Ben had gone away, he too. In the room a cupboard, big as a closet, was still packed with his toys: clockwork cars, tractors, a farm and its animals, cowboy belts and hats, spurs and pistols. There were at least twenty pistols of all kinds, all broken.

Ben never threw anything away. It was he who hoarded his old toys in the cupboard, and one day not long ago his father had caught him solemnly trying to play a tune on a ten-cent whistle that dated from his ninth or tenth year.

A loud-speaker, out there on the sports field, was giving a running commentary on the game, and the people on the benches must be talking about him. Had Musak listened to the radio? Or perhaps someone had come and told him the news? Just the same, he would be sitting on his porch, smoking his patched-up pipe, which whistled when he sucked.

A car pulled up in front of the shop, two people got out, two men, to judge by their footsteps, who went to the window and looked inside.

"Isn't there a bell?" one of them asked.

"I don't see one."

There was a knock on the glass pane of the door. Dave did not move. Then one of the men stepped back into the middle of the street to look at the second-floor windows.

The old Polish woman must have been leaning out of her own, because they shouted to her from below:

"Mr. Galloway, please?"

"The next window."

"Is he home?"

Half in English, half in her own language, she tried to explain to them that you had to go around the building, enter by the small door between the garages, and go upstairs. They apparently understood, because finally they left.

Dave knew that at any moment they would be knocking at his door and did not even ask himself who they were.

It was time, in any case, for him to emerge from his torpor. It had worn off by degrees and, in the end, he had been obliged to maintain it artificially. The thing was a trick, a certain way of tensing his muscles as he bore down on the mattress. He did not wait to hear footsteps on the stairs before raising his head and opening his eyes, and it was strange to rediscover his everyday background, the objects with their exact shape, the bright square of the window, a corner of the living room that he could see through the half-open doorway.

There was a knock and, without answering, he sat on the edge of the bed, his mind still vacant, without having fully regained awareness of the drama that was unfolding.

"Mr. Galloway!"

The knocking grew louder. The neighbor, having emerged from her apartment, was talking volubly.

"I heard him come in about one o'clock and I'm sure he hasn't gone out again. What's so strange is that since then I haven't heard any sound in his apartment."

"Do you think he's the sort of man who would commit suicide?" asked another voice.

He knitted his eyebrows, astounded, because this idea had never for a moment occurred to him.

"Mr. Galloway! Do you hear?"

Resignedly he got up, went to the door, and unlocked it.

"Yes?" he said.

They were not police. One of them had a leather case slung from his shoulder and a big camera in his hand.

The stouter of the two gave the name of a New York newspaper, as though there were no need of any further explanation.

"Get your picture, Johnny."

He explained by way of apology:

"That way it'll arrive in time for the evening edition."

They didn't wait for his permission. There was a white flash, a click.

"Wait a minute! Where were you when we arrived?"

He answered without thinking, because he was not in the habit of lying:

"In my son's room."

He regretted it instantly, too late.

"That room there? Would you mind going back in for a moment? Like that, yes. Stand in front of the bed. Look down at it."

Another car pulled up in front of the house, a door slammed, there were hurried footsteps on the sidewalk.

"Hurry up! Got it? Rush it to the office. Don't worry about me. I'll fix some way of getting back. Excuse me, Mr. Galloway, but we were here first and there's no reason why we shouldn't have first chance."

Two more men thrust their way into the apartment, of which the door was no longer locked. All four knew one another, chatted among themselves while they looked around.

"From what we've been told, the state police brought you back here about one o'clock and you hadn't eaten. Haven't you had anything to eat since?"

He said no. He felt powerless before their energy. They seemed so much stronger than he, so sure of themselves!

"Aren't you hungry?"

He no longer knew. This noise, these comings and goings, these lights that flashed every minute were making him dizzy.

"Was it you who cooked the meals for your son and yourself?"

It was now that he wanted to weep, not from grief, but from weariness.

"I don't know," he answered. "I don't even know what you want of me."

"Have you got a picture of him?"

He nearly gave himself away, said no, fiercely, resolved, this time, to defend himself. It was a lie. There was an album filled with pictures of Ben in a drawer in his bedroom. At all costs they must not be allowed to know.

"You should eat something."

"Perhaps."

"Would you like one of us to make you a sandwich?"

He preferred to do it himself and was photographed again in front of the open refrigerator.

"Do they still not know where he is?" he asked in his turn, timidly, ready to draw back.

"You haven't been listening to the radio?"

He was ashamed of having to admit it, as though he had failed in his duty as a father.

"From now on, the police aren't relying on the information that's coming in, because the blue Oldsmobile has been reported from five or six different places at the same time. Some people claim to have seen it an hour ago near Harrisburg, and that'd mean they've backtracked. On the other hand, a restaurant keeper in Union Bridge, Virginia, says he served them breakfast before he heard their description over the radio. He's even given details of the meal they ordered: shrimps and fried chicken."

He tried to keep his face expressionless. It was Ben's favorite meal whenever they ate in a restaurant.

"I suppose it was your automatic they took with them?"

He protested, relieved by the diversion:

"I've never owned any kind of weapon."

"Did you know he had one?"

They were taking notes. Galloway, still standing, tried to eat his sandwich while he drank a glass of milk.

"I never knew him to have anything but toy pistols. He was a quiet boy."

It was for Ben's sake that he was enduring this. He wanted to avoid setting the newspapers against him and so he was patient with the reporters, doing his best to please them.

"Did he play a lot with pistols?"

"No more than other boys."

"Up till what age?"

"I don't know. Twelve, maybe."

"And after that, what games did he play?"

He was incapable of remembering, like that, at point-blank range, and this embarrassed him. It seemed to him that he should have been able to remember everything that concerned his son. Wasn't that the time when he went crazy about football? No. The football phase, that had come at least a year later. There had been an interim period.

"Animals!" he exclaimed.

"What animals?"

"All kinds. Anything he could get hold of. He kept white mice, young rabbits he caught in the fields and that died after a few days. . . ."

This did not seem to interest them.

"His mother died when he was very young?"

"I'd rather not talk about that."

"Look, Mr. Galloway, if we don't talk about it, other people will. Within the next hour, other reporters will probably have got here. And what you don't tell them, they'll find out elsewhere."

It was true. It was better to help them.

"She isn't dead."

"Divorced?"

He murmured reluctantly, as though he were surrendering a part of his secret life:

"She left me."

"How old was the kid?"

"Six months. But I'd so much rather——"

"Don't be afraid we won't be tactful."

They were doing their job, Dave realized, and he bore them no grudge. Like everyone else, he had read stories of this sort in the papers, but it had never occurred to him to put himself in the place of the people they were about. Those things had seemed to happen in a separate world.

"You knew about his affair with Lillian Hawkins?"

He said no, because it was the truth.

"Did you know her?"

"By sight. She came to my shop two or three times."

"I take it you and your son were great friends?"

How could he answer them? He said yes. That was his conviction. At the very least it had been his conviction until the previous night and he could not yet bring himself to abandon it. One of his interviewers, tall and thin, looked more like a young Harvard professor than a reporter, and it worried Dave to feel his eyes upon him. This one had not yet asked him anything and, when at length he spoke, it was to say:

"In fact, you've been both a father and a mother to your son."

"I've done my best."

"It didn't ever occur to you that by marrying again you might have given him a more normal life?"

He blushed, felt himself blushing, and was all the more unhappy. Without thinking he stammered:

"No."

As though he were pursuing a definite line of thought, the reporter continued, implacably:

"Were you jealous of him?"

"Jealous?" he repeated.

"If he'd asked you for permission to marry Lillian Hawkins, how would you have reacted?"

"I don't know."

"Would you have given it?"

"I suppose so."

"Willingly?"

One of the others, the stout one, who had been the first to arrive, gave his colleague a slight nudge with his elbow and he beat a retreat.

"I'm sorry if I've pressed you too far, but you see, it's the human angle that interests me."

The Everton team must have scored a home run, because there was a burst of cheering that lasted several minutes.

"How did you hear the news?"

"From the police. First they tried to call me up. The telephone's down below, in the shop."

On this subject he was quite ready to give them all the details. It was a relief to him. He explained in far too many words how he had to walk around the building to get to his shop and how two uniformed patrolmen had appeared from their car and read his name over the window, then had consulted their notebook.

"You'd no idea what was coming?"

They talked together in low voices. After which the photographer asked:

"Would it bother you to come and pose for a moment in your shop?"

He agreed, still for Ben's sake. He was a little ashamed of the part they were making him play but he would have done anything to gain their favor.

They went down in single file and Dave, who had forgotten the key of the shop, had to go back to get it. The apartment, where all the men had been smoking, no longer had the same odor and had lost its intimacy.

It was only at that moment, while he was gazing around the room looking for the key, that he realized that a certain life was finally ended and that, whatever happened, the existence he had shared with Ben between those walls would never be resumed.

This was no longer his home, their home. The objects it contained had no identity and Ben's bed, on which he, Dave, had been stretched a little while ago, was no longer anything but an ordinary bed bearing the impress of a body.

In the yard they were talking about him in undertones. They must be feeling sorry for him. The one like a professor had hurt him unintentionally with his questions, because he had spoken words that henceforth would torment him. No doubt he would have thought of it for himself. He had already thought of it, before what had happened, but not in the same way. Expressed in a certain way, the truth became disturbing, sordid, like the photographs of women in certain poses that young men surreptitiously pass around.

Someone asked him from below:

"Did you find it?"

He picked up the key and went downstairs, then they all walked together.

"Is that your garage?"

"Yes."

"Get a picture of it later on, Dick. We'll probably have the whole center spread to fill."

Two women seated on the grass were keeping an eye, while they gossiped, on the children playing around them and they watched from a distance as the group went into the shop. One of them, the younger, was pregnant.

"What are the hooks for?"

"That's where I hang the watches under repair, during the day. It takes several days to regulate a watch."

"You work at this bench, do you? Where are the watches?"

"In the safe."

They asked him to hang them on the hooks, to put on his white smock, and to fix the black-ringed magnifying glass in his right eye.

"Could you hold a tool in your hand? . . . Yes . . . like that. . . . Don't move."

He pretended to be working.

"Hold it one second more. I'll take another."

He should have had someone to protect him, and the thought of his father passed through his mind. He hadn't the courage to resist them, submissively did everything they told him, so much so that his readiness to co-operate surprised them.

Was he entitled to lock himself in and see no one? Just now, if he had not let them in, they would no doubt have gone for a locksmith or else broken the door down for fear he had hanged himself!

"Have you found any photos of the girl in your son's belongings?"

"I haven't searched his belongings."

"Aren't you going to?"

"Certainly not."

He had never opened Ben's wallet, not even the time, when he was eleven, when a dollar had vanished from the cash drawer. It was in any case, so far as he knew, the only time this had happened. He had spoken of it to his son without pursuing the matter. Just two sentences, in a sorrowful voice.

His own mother, when he was young, had been in the habit of going through his drawers and his pockets and he had never forgiven her for it.

"Have the police searched the place?"

He stared at them, horrified.

"Do you think they will?"

"It's more than likely. I'm surprised they haven't done it already."

When all was said, what did it matter? After his father's death they had stacked part of the furniture on the porch encircling the house, and the rest on the lawn, and people had come long distances to examine it, to sniff and poke at everything. The auction had taken place on a Saturday and had been interrupted while lemonade and hot dogs were served to everyone there. They had sold everything, including frames that still contained photographs.

He had not been allowed to see his father in his coffin, lest it should frighten him, but no one had thought of preventing him from being present at that carnage.

It was something rather similar that was now happening, after all. All their private life would be brought out into the open, their intimacy exposed, their past, their habits, their smallest doings and gestures discussed by the public.

What they did not know was that, while they were questioning him in this fashion and making him pose for photographs, he was more with Ben than with them. Throughout that afternoon he had had in his mind's eye, like an overprint, a picture of the red soil of Virginia, the trees taller, more stately, with darker foliage than the ones here, and he had thought of the blue car speeding along the side roads.

They would have to stop somewhere. Would they run the risk of spending the night at a motel, or would they drive the car into some wood to sleep there?

They didn't have much money. Dave had mechanically calculated the amount, that morning, when the lieutenant had told him of the twelve or fourteen dollars in Charles Ralston's wallet. With the thirty-eight dollars Lillian had taken from her parents' kitchen, this made roughly fifty dollars. If Ben, in addition, had saved as many as ten . . .

They had to eat, to buy gasoline several times a day.

It was at this moment that the reporter whose questions had disturbed him said:

"Tell me, Mr. Galloway, has it occurred to you that you might be able to send him a message?"

He gazed at him in astonishment, not understanding.

"I represent the Associated Press. Your message would be sent out by teletype to every newspaper in the States and I'm certain they would all print it. It's likely, too, that your son will have the curiosity to buy papers as he goes, if only to get some idea of which way the search is heading."

He had seen that Dave was hesitating and perhaps had anticipated his thoughts. Otherwise why should he have added:

"It would be better for him, don't you think?"

Galloway recalled the words one nearly always reads on criminal notices displayed in the post offices.

"Warning! This man is armed."

Ben also was armed. Which meant that the police, rather than run risks, would be tempted to shoot first.

Was that what the reporter was suggesting? That he should advise Ben to give himself up?

"Let's go back to your apartment, shall we?"

It was better to do so, because the baseball game had just finished and the first cars were passing. The crowd would follow in a stream, as when they came out of church or a movie. Dave, preoccupied with this new idea that had just been implanted in his mind, nearly forgot to slip the spring lock on the door.

The plump reporter, the first to arrive, stood, hesitating at the corner of the alleyway.

"How does one get to the Hawkins place?"

"You turn left at the garage, then you take the first on the right."

Evidently considering that he had got as much out of Galloway as there was to get, he went off to question them in their turn. The other, however, seemed to take no interest in Lillian, but only in Ben and his father. He was cold and understanding at the same time. The photographer also left them, stood waiting for the crowd to come in order to photograph them outside the shop.

Back in the apartment the representative of the Associated Press said in a detached voice:

"The police know as well as you do how much money your son has in his pocket. It's easy to figure out what it's costing them to travel by road. They reckon that by tomorrow evening they'll have come to the end of their cash."

"Did the lieutenant tell you that?"

"Not him. The FBI, which is taking part in the search, knows that they've crossed one or more state borders in the car. I have to apologize for——"

"It's all right."

"Maybe if your son read in the newspaper that you begged him to give himself up . . ."

"I understand."

"Take your time before you decide. I don't want you to blame yourself afterwards. It's not as if he could hope to reach a foreign country. And, even if he did, he would come under the extradition laws, whether it was Canada or Mexico."

The reporter had stationed himself in front of the window and was staring at the trees across the way, at the children who had left the baseball field and were running across the grass.

The police would shoot first; Dave was convinced of it. The reporter wasn't trying to trick him. No doubt he knew more about the FBI's plans than he was allowed to say.

He was tempted, to the point of being overtaken by a sort of giddiness. And it was not only with the idea of preventing his son from being killed. For no precise reason, simply by intuition, he didn't believe in that possibility. It existed in theory. It seemed logical, almost inevitable. Nevertheless he could have sworn that things would not happen that way.

It wasn't possible that he wouldn't again see Ben alive.

His companion still stood with his back to him, as though to avoid influencing him, Dave got out his handkerchief, wiped his forehead, the palms of his hands. Twice, before speaking, he opened his mouth.

"I'll do it," he said finally.

And his hands trembled at the thought that in a sense he was going to make contact with Ben.

5

Others had come: five, it seemed to him, each accompanied by a photographer, and one had brought his wife, who waited below in an open car. For one reason or another there were more than five cars, some with the name of the paper painted on the doors, parked in front of the house, and people went incessantly up and down the stairs; the door remained open almost all the time. One of the photographers, who found that the smoke interfered with his work, went and opened the window and the draft made the curtains tremble, and the leaves of the writing pads. People talked, smoked, moved in every corner.

Each asked more or less the same questions and Dave was answering mechanically, without trying to think, with the feeling that all this was no longer of any importance. His knees were shaking with fatigue, but he could not bring himself to sit down, remained standing in the midst of them, facing now this way and now that.

In the street groups passed slowly along the opposite sidewalk, bordering the lawn, couples walking arm in arm, families with children going in front or being led by the hand, and everyone looked up to try to see in through the window; some stopped altogether. As for the boys and girls who ordinarily hung around outside Mack's, they had set up their headquarters around the press cars.

Twice Dave had seen in the distance a patrolman of that morning, one of the two in uniform, the one who hadn't left the town and seemed busy.

Without noticing it he smoked cigarette after cigarette, because those who questioned him offered him their packs, and they didn't look around for the ash tray any more, just dropped the stubs on the floor and crushed them with their heels.

The sky, by six o'clock, was overcast, the weather had become oppressive, as though a storm were approaching, and occasionally a sharp gust of wind shook the leaves of the trees opposite.

They had ended by going away one after the other. All went sooner or later to the Hawkins house, which must have been in the same state of disorder. Some went to the Old Barn to telephone their stories.

At the moment when Galloway fancied himself at last alone and was about to sink into his armchair there was yet another knock on the door and he went to open it, found a man carrying a suitcase that seemed very heavy.

"Have they all gone?" he asked in astonishment.

He put down the case, mopped his forehead.

"I represent a radio network. A short time ago, the appeal you made to your son was sent in to us, for our news bulletin. My chiefs and I thought it would be more likely to make an impression on him if he heard your own voice."

What Dave had mistaken for a suitcase was a tape recorder, which the network man was setting up on one of the tables. He looked around for a power outlet.

"Do you mind if I close the window a minute?"

Dave's message had been difficult to word and, like Ruth fifteen and a half years before, he had torn up several drafts. At the time he had been alone in the apartment with the journalist who was like a professor and the latter had kept discreetly in the background all the time he was writing, without offering a single suggestion.

None of the phrases he had tried had given him the feeling of making contact with his son.

"Your father urges you . . ."

That would not do. He knew what he wanted to say, but the words were lacking. Since they had never been separated, Ben and he, they had never had occasion to write to one another, except notes that one of them might leave on the kitchen table.

"Back in an hour. Have your dinner, there's some cold meat in the refrigerator."

He had wished this were as simple.

"Ben, I implore you . . ." he wrote.

It did not matter if other people laughed or failed to understand. He was talking to no one but his son.

"Ben, I implore you, give yourself up."

He had nearly handed over the sheet of paper without adding any more, then he had taken it back and scribbled:

"I'm not angry with you."

He had signed it, "Dad."

The representative of the Associated Press had read it, had raised his eyes toward Galloway, who was watching him and expecting some criticism.

"Can I say that?"

He thought he was going to be asked to delete the last words. Instead, almost solemnly, the man folded the sheet of paper and put it in his wallet.

"You certainly can!"

He had said it in an odd voice and he shook him by the hand before leaving.

Now Dave asked the network man:

"Do you want me to use the same words?"

"The same ones or fresh ones if you like."

He set the tape recorder going, tested it, began his introduction in the manner of a professional broadcaster.

"Now, ladies and gentlemen, we are interrupting our program for a moment to relay a message that Mr. Galloway, from his apartment in Everton, is going to send over the air to his son. We can only hope, like all of you, that his son is listening."

He held out the microphone, motioned to Dave to speak.

"This is Dad, Ben. . . ."

At that moment his eyes filled with tears and the outline of the microphone grew blurred; he vaguely perceived the gesture of the other man urging him to continue.

"It's better for you to give yourself up. . . . Yes . . . I honestly think it's better. . . . I'll always be on your side, no matter what happens. . . ."

His voice became stifled and he was only just able to finish:

"I'm not angry with you. . . ."

The network man turned off the tape recorder.

"Very good. Fine. Do you want to hear yourself?"

He shook his head. The blue Oldsmobile had a radio. It was probable that Ben and Lillian were on the alert for every news bulletin.

"What time will it go out?" he managed to ask as his visitor moved toward the door.

"Probably in the nine-o'clock bulletin."

It wasn't in order to hear his own voice, but so that, when the time came, he might be near Ben in thought.

Before sitting down he went and opened the window again, indifferent to the procession in the street, to the curiosity he aroused in the town and everywhere else.

By half-past seven the clouds were so dark and low that he had to turn on the light, and it was then that he received another visit, that of an FBI man, in plain clothes, who was not more than thirty years old and whom he seemed to have seen before.

"I must apologize for bothering you after the day you've had, but believe me, Mr. Galloway, I wouldn't trouble you if it weren't absolutely necessary."

He held out an official document, at which Dave merely glanced. It was a search warrant.

"I'd like to examine your son's possessions. Is that his room on the left?"

Dave did not ask what he was looking for, noted that it was Ben's papers, letters, exercise books that principally interested his visitor.

"Sometime I'll have to ask you for as complete a list as possible of your son's friends, including those who may have left the district. Have you relatives in the South or West, Mr. Galloway?"

"Some aunts, in Virginia . . . if they're still alive. I haven't seen them since I was six and I've never heard from them."

"You've never been to the Middle West with your son?"

"The only places we've been to together are Cape Cod and New York."

"You know, it's unusual for anyone to start out by road the way he has done without having a definite objective. If we knew what that objective was, it would obviously narrow the field of search."

He spoke as though he took it for granted that Dave was on their side.

"The idea of making for one place rather than another could be derived from various sources, from something he'd read or from a movie, or again from a conversation with a friend."

Ben possessed few books other than his schoolbooks. There were only two shelves of them in a small bookcase and for the most part they were the animal books that had interested him four years ago.

Why did Dave feel the need to say, as though he were being accused, or as though he wanted to make a good impression:

"You know, it isn't here that he got the weapon. I've never owned one."

He had said it already that morning. He repeated it.

"We've found out where the automatic came from."

While he went on leafing through the books the FBI man explained:

"I suppose you know Dr. Van Horn?"

"Very well. He's our doctor. His son Jimmy has played in this room for years."

It had happened more especially just before Ben went to high school. Jimmy Van Horn, at that time, had been small and thin, of an astonishing vivacity. Then suddenly, two years ago, he had started to grow in height and now he was half a head taller than any of his schoolfellows, seemed embarrassed by his size, by his voice, which had been very late in starting to break.

"Have you seen him lately?"

"He hasn't been here, if that's what you mean, but I've every reason to believe that Ben often sees him."

"Dr. Van Horn bought an automatic twelve years ago, when he was still living in Albany and was often called out at night to visit places in the outer districts. It was this weapon, almost forgotten in a drawer, that Jimmy sold to your son for five dollars. He admitted it this afternoon to one of the highway patrolmen. The deal took place a week ago."

Dave had no comment to make. The Van Horns passed for wealthy people, possessed the handsomest house in Everton, surrounded by large grounds. Each of the girls had her own horse; Mrs. Van Horn was the heiress of a manufacturer of chemical products whose trademark was known from coast to coast.

"Was it you who bought this booklet?"

He was shown an almanac that he didn't remember having seen before in the apartment. The general-information section contained a list of former presidents of the United States, population figures for the big towns, statistics, the speed limits imposed in the different states.

It was on another page that the agent found, almost instantly, as though he had been looking for them, two penciled crosses.

The first column on this page bore a list of the states in alphabetical order; parallel columns gave the minimum ages at which marriage licenses were granted, first for men, then for women, and another column gave the number of days' notice required.

"I'm afraid I'll have to take this booklet with me."

"May I see it?"

The two states marked with a cross were Illinois and Mississippi. In Illinois the minimum age for boys was eighteen, for girls sixteen, while in Mississippi the figures were fourteen and twelve respectively. Neither state required notice, so that it was possible to go to the house of any justice of the peace and be married in a few minutes. Ben looked eighteen.

"I don't think I'll need the list of names I asked you for just now. This seems to me to answer the question."

"You think they're making for one of those states? It would have been so simple to——"

He broke off. It was not for him to pretend not to understand.

"I'm sure," he went on, "that when he explains to us . . ."

The other looked at him curiously, as though he had said some-thing enormous.

"You should try to get some rest, Mr. Galloway. Tomorrow will probably be a hard day."

He, too, shook him by the hand. Dave was almost tempted to try to keep him back, terrified, suddenly, at the thought of being left alone. He no longer knew where to put himself in the apart-ment, which so many people had invaded and now had no more intimacy than a station waiting room. The very lamps seemed to give less light than usual.

Should he have made sure, before the police searched it, that there was nothing in Ben's room that could put them on the track? It seemed to him that he had failed his son, for lack of astuteness, and he wanted to ask his forgiveness. Who knows? Perhaps he had also been wrong to write his message, to send out his appeal over the radio. People were certain to think that he had done so in order to put himself on the side of the law.

But please, God, don't let Ben think that! Dave had not thought of it until then. The idea suddenly occurred to him and he was filled with remorse; he would have liked to take back the message he had written and later naïvely repeated into the tape recorder.

It wasn't true! He was not trying to show himself in a favorable light, or to evade his responsibilities. Ben was himself; he was ready to stand judgment in his stead and to accept the punishment.

Would Ben understand this when he heard, "I'm not angry with you"?

On the spur of the moment he had been able to find no other words. These were the only ones that had come to his lips. Only now did he begin to realize that they implied a degree of accusa-tion.

He was not accusing, not explaining, either. Later on would be the time to try to explain.

Ben was his son and Ben couldn't have changed from one day to the next. Even when he thought of Charles Ralston lying at the side of the road and of the scene that must have taken place in the car, he could not bring himself to reproach Ben. He was simply hor-rified, as one is by a cataclysm.

It exhausted him to think. He would have liked to be able to stop the little wheels of his mind as one stops the mechanism of a clock.

Outside large drops of rain were falling more and more rapidly, but it was not thundering; there was no lightning to be seen. Dave was at loose ends. His thoughts were at loose ends too. It was only a quarter-past eight and his radio message would not be broadcast until nine.

He was on the point of going out of doors, bareheaded, so that the cold rain might refresh him, and it was a relief, this time, to hear footsteps on the stairs.

Someone came up, making as little noise as possible, then whoever it was stood outside the door, without knocking, without saying anything, while, inside, he waited in suspense.

A good minute passed before he heard a soft rustling on the floor. Someone was slipping a sheet of paper under the door and it was so mysterious that he hesitated a minute before picking it up.

The message had been written with a thick pencil such as carpenters use:

"If you don't want to see me, don't open the door. I'll leave a little package on the landing."

It was signed, "Frank," Musak's Christian name, which no one ever used. He was waiting and when Dave opened the door he found him standing in the half darkness, with a package in his hand.

"I thought maybe you wouldn't want to see anyone, or that you were asleep."

"Come in, Musak."

He was the first person, that day, to wipe his feet on the mat, and for the first time he could remember Galloway saw him take off his cap.

During all the years they had known one another, and had played backgammon every Saturday, Musak had never come up to the apartment because, when he had anything to say to his friend, it was in the shop that he always stopped.

"I brought this," he said, pulling the paper wrapping off a bottle of rye.

He had remembered something Dave had once said to him: that, because of Ben, he never kept liquor in the house, both for the example and so as not to put temptation in his way.

"When you want me to go, you only have to say so."

He seemed even bigger and rougher here than in his own home and yet he moved without a sound, almost without causing a stir in the air, as he might have done in a sickroom. He found glasses in the kitchen cupboard, got ice cubes from the refrigerator.

"Have you had anything to eat?"

Dave nodded.

"What?"

"A sandwich."

"When?"

"I don't know. The baseball game hadn't finished."

He recalled the shouting on the ground while he had the sandwich in his hand.

Musak held out one of the two glasses and he could not refuse.

"It's time you had something more solid. Sit down. Leave it to me."

He talked in his grumbling voice, less loud than usual, went back into the kitchen, again opened the refrigerator, where he found two large steaks.

Every Saturday Dave bought two thick steaks for Sunday dinner, for Ben and himself. And this tradition was more than ten years old. Only when he saw the meat on a plate did he reflect that yesterday had been Saturday, and that, at about ten in the morning, as he had done so many times before, he had shut his shop to go and do his marketing at the First National Store.

The notice he left on the door read:

"Back in a quarter of an hour."

That afternoon, at about five, he had been working on a woman's watch when Ben had come into the shop. Although Dave had had his back turned, he had known it was his son, from the way he opened the door.

"You won't mind if I don't come in for supper, Dad?"

Dave had not turned, had remained, with the glass in his right eye, bent over the movement of the watch. No doubt he had said:

"Don't be too late."

It was his usual phrase.

"You going to Musak's?" Ben had asked.

This had not seemed to him out of the way. Ben had probably asked the same question on other Saturdays.

"Yes. I'll be back around half-past eleven."

"Night, Dad."

Galloway suddenly called:

"Musak!"

"What?"

"I can't eat anything."

The steak continued nevertheless to splutter on the cooker.

"They asked me to send out an appeal over the radio for him to give himself up."

The cabinetmaker gave him a curious glance from the kitchen, contented himself with saying:

"Yes."

"I agreed. They recorded it."

Musak made no comment.

"I'm wondering now if I was right."

It was raining hard. The raindrops rattled on the roof. He went to shut the window because a puddle was beginning to form on the floor.

"I was afraid they'd kill him."

"Come and sit here."

Musak had laid a place for him on a napkin, not knowing where the tablecloths were kept, and, seated opposite Galloway, with his elbows on the table, he waited as one does when persuading a child to eat.

"I listened to the radio all afternoon," he muttered.

"What are they saying?"

"They're repeating almost the same words every hour. Their idea now is that the car's heading for Chicago. But there are people who claim they've seen it on the roads in South Carolina."

Almost without realizing it Dave had begun to eat, and Musak, for his part, had poured himself a second glass of whisky.

"A state police officer spent the day questioning people in town. He came to see me."

"To confirm that we were together last night?"

"Yes. And there are two reporters still here; they've taken rooms at the Old Barn."

It was the first time since that morning that Galloway had relaxed, without knowing it. Musak's presence was comforting. It did him good to hear his voice, to see his gross, familiar face.

"Would you like some apple pie? I saw some in the refrigerator."

The apple pie was also part of the Sunday menu.

"Won't you have some?"

"I had supper."

He lit his pipe instead, the one he had mended with wire, and for an instant, because of the acrid smell of the tobacco, Dave thought himself in the yellow house at the end of the lane.

"Do you mean to listen at nine o'clock?"

Galloway nodded and Musak looked at his old silver watch, which had never needed mending.

"We've got plenty of time. There's still twelve minutes to go."

When Galloway rose to take his plate into the kitchen, he stopped him:

"We'll do that later."

He pointed to his armchair, as though he knew his habits.

"Coffee?"

Without awaiting a reply, he went to make some, huge and silent, and not even the rattle of a cup was to be heard.

Dave glanced at his own watch and grew more nervous as the time approached. At five minutes to nine, he went to get the radio from Ben's room, plugged it into one of the outlets in the living room, and turned the knob to give it time to warm up.

Musak had poured out coffee for himself as well. They heard the end of a symphony. Then, after a commercial, the latest news of the day was announced.

It did not start with Ben, but with a declaration by the President on the subject of tariffs, then went on to a frontier incident in Palestine.

The announcer was speaking rapidly, with a staccato delivery, not making a pause as he passed from one topic to the next.

"On the national scene: the police of six states, joined by the FBI, are still searching for the sixteen-year-old killer, Ben Galloway. With his girl friend, Lillian Hawkins, aged fifteen and a half, Galloway left Everton in New York State, on Saturday evening, driving his father's car. After killing a man named Charles Ralston, aged fifty-four, from Long Eddy, with a bullet from an automatic, near the Pennsylvania border, the couple took possession of the victim's blue Oldsmobile and continued to drive in a southwesterly direction."

The two men, motionless, avoided each other's eyes. Contrary to his expectation Dave was more impatient than moved, as though the event, recounted in this fashion, no longer concerned either him or his son.

"The car, New York license number 4D-8795, has been reported successively in Pennsylvania, Virginia, and, according to the latest news, Ohio. It is, however, difficult to determine the exact route taken by the fugitives, owing to the large number of contradictory reports that are reaching the police."

Another voice took over.

"And now, ladies and gentlemen, we are interrupting our news bulletin for a moment to broadcast an appeal that Mr. Dave Galloway is making to his son."

It was the voice of the network man who came on earlier, but it seemed to Galloway that the words were not quite the same.

There was a pause, then a scratching sound, and then with a strange resonance, as though they were spoken in the resounding emptiness of a cathedral, came the words that were familiar to him but that, all of a sudden, made him feel ashamed.

" 'This is Dad, Ben. . . . It's better for you to give yourself up. . . .' "

The pauses between the sentences seemed interminable.

" 'Yes . . . I honestly think it's better. . . . I'll always be on your side, no matter what happens. . . .' "

He heard himself breathe very hard, and pause as though he were asking someone's permission to continue, before ending:

" 'I'm not angry with you.' "

"And now, ladies and gentlemen, here is the latest weather forecast. . . ."

He reached out his hand to turn it off. Musak said nothing. Galloway had no wish to speak either and now hoped that Ben was not listening.

If he were listening, somewhere on the road, his eyes intent on the track of the headlights, wouldn't he too have already turned it off?

"I thought . . ." began Dave.

He had thought he was acting for the best. He had imagined he would be making contact with Ben. He had received them all politely. He had answered their questions, accepted their cigarettes.

He had betrayed his son, it was only now that he realized it. He had seemed to be excusing himself, coming to their help.

Did Musak understand what he felt? In silence he drank a mouthful of rye and wiped his lips. A crash of thunder sounded, so loud that the lightning might have struck one of the trees opposite or the belfry of the Catholic church. It was not followed by any other. For several minutes the rain doubled in intensity, set up a real pandemonium on the roof, after which, suddenly, it ceased as though by magic and there was silence.

Dave had let his head sink a little on his chest, but, tired though he was, he did not sleep, did not doze, continued to reproach himself. When he saw Musak get up, he took no notice, nor of the sound of the tap in the kitchen.

The police of six states . . .

And they were two children in the car, glancing in terror at the cars that overtook or passed them, gazing into the darkness of the night in constant apprehension of seeing a police barrier rise up ahead of them.

The FBI man had taken away the almanac in which two crosses designated Illinois and Mississippi.

Were they still intent upon the same objective as they wound blindly between the traps? Were they continuing this mad flight simply in order that, having crossed a given frontier, they might rush to a justice of the peace and cry to him, panting:

"Marry us!"

They might, if they had not made too many detours, reach Illinois that same night, perhaps were there already. It was not improbable that, in some remote village, they would arouse some elderly judge who had not listened to the radio all day.

Were they, too, having to pass through storms, down there on the plains of the Middle West? He regretted not having listened to the weather forecast, began to grow restless, wished Musak would come back and sit opposite him to prevent him from thinking. He, too, was on the highway, with the monotonous sound of the windshield wipers seeming to tick off the seconds.

The police of six states . . . plus the FBI.

He got up suddenly to pour himself a mouthful of whisky, gazed at the radio, calculating that there were still thirty-five minutes to go before the ten-o'clock bulletin. He had a feeling that this time there would be news.

"You shouldn't have washed up, Musak."

The other shrugged his shoulders, poured himself a drink, and sat down in an armchair.

"Don't forget I'll go whenever you want me to."

Dave shook his head. He didn't want him to go. He dared not imagine what that evening would have been like if Musak hadn't come and humbly slipped a sheet of paper under the door.

"People don't know, they can't know," Galloway said as though to himself.

And Musak murmured, as though he, too, were talking to himself:

"When my daughter ran away, it was a year and a half before I had any news of her."

It was the first time he had ever made any allusion to his private life and no doubt it was to come to the aid of his friend.

"In the end I had a letter from a hospital in Baltimore where she ended up, without any money, and was expecting a baby."

"What did you do?"

"I went there. She refused to see me. I left some money with the office and left."

He said no more and Dave didn't venture to ask whether he had seen her again later, or if this was the daughter who wrote to him now and then from California and sent him snapshots of her children.

"I wonder what they're thinking. . . ."

His thoughts were still with the couple in the car.

"Everyone thinks differently," sighed Musak.

He added after a moment, during which the whistle of his pipe could be heard:

"Everyone figures he's right."

Galloway looked at his watch, impatient to hear the radio.

"You should sit down."

"I know. I've been on my feet nearly all day. I can't help it."

Every time he sat down a fit of trembling overcame his legs, a nervous twinge spread through his body. He said suddenly:

"Dr. Van Horn must be awfully upset."

He did not explain why, although he realized from Musak's expression that he had not heard the story of the automatic.

"In a moment you will hear the latest news."

The commercial was given first.

"During the last few minutes we have learned that Ben Galloway, the sixteen-year-old killer, whose father broadcast an appeal to him in our last bulletin . . ."

They held their breath.

". . . arrived with his companion, at about the time of that appeal, at the home of a justice of the peace in Brownsville, on the Indiana-Illinois border, and asked him to marry them immediately. The judge, who had chanced to hear a description of the couple over the radio a short time previously, left the room on the pretext of getting the necessary papers and rushed to the telephone.

"Before he could get through to the sheriff, the sound of the car's engine told him that the two young people, no doubt guessing what he intended to do, had made a dash for it.

"In any event, this narrows the area of search. It also indicates that the blue Oldsmobile had covered a lot more ground, in the past twenty-four hours, than had hitherto been supposed and that Ben Galloway can scarcely have left the wheel.

"The Illinois state police are watching all crossroads and it seems that an early arrest may be expected."

Had Musak noticed? At a certain moment, during the broadcast, Galloway had not been able to prevent a slight, scarcely perceptible smile from rising to his lips. It was not a smile of satisfaction, or of irony. It signified nothing precise. Only a sort of contact with Ben, out there. He shut his eyes to recapture the feeling, but, like a breath of air, it had already passed, subtle, impalpable.

There remained only two men in their armchairs.

6

That night was a little like a night one spends on a train, at times dozing, at times plunged in exhausted slumber through which one is nevertheless conscious of the rhythm of the wheels, of the stations where one pulls up with a hiss of steam while unknown voices call from one platform to another.

When, for example, Musak touched him on the shoulder, he knew that he was in his armchair and not in bed, and that he was being awakened for the midnight news. He wondered whether Musak had fallen asleep too, did not venture to ask, rubbed his eyes, saw that the whisky had sunk to a lower level in the bottle. The tubes in the radio were already warming up, voices came out of the silence, growing so loud that the volume had to be reduced.

It was the end of a play. A man and a woman were resolving to patch up their life together as best they could. He did not notice the commercial.

"Ladies and gentlemen, as we announced a quarter of an hour ago in a special bulletin . . ."

Neither Musak nor he had thought that there might be a special announcement and they had turned on the radio at only the usual times.

". . . the hunt for the sixteen-year-old murderer, Ben Galloway, which has gone on for nearly twenty-four hours, came to an end this evening, a little before eleven o'clock, at a farm in Indiana, where the couple sought to take refuge using the threat of an automatic. Shots were exchanged with the police and a sergeant was wounded by a bullet in the hip. Ben Galloway and his fifteen-and-a-half-year-old companion, Lillian Hawkins, both uninjured, have been taken to Indianapolis."

Was Musak perhaps a little surprised by his friend's reaction? Galloway uttered a sigh that resembled one of relief, his nerves instantly relaxed, and he stood up, rubbed his eyes as he looked about him with an air of disgust, as though sickened by the atmosphere in which he had been immersed since the morning.

It was over. He had no more need to wait, to stay there as though in suspense. His first thought was that before leaving he had to have a bath and shave, because he had a feeling that he smelled unpleasantly of sweat.

"I'm going down to the shop to call up the airport," he said.

It seemed to him natural. He was going to see Ben; he would talk to him. Ben would explain everything, would tell him the whole truth because, to his knowledge, his son had never lied to him.

He was a little irritated that Musak came down with him. He no longer needed anyone. Everything was quite simple now; he would take the first plane to Indianapolis and he would see Ben.

Down in the shop Musak, going ahead of him, took the phone, saying:

"It's better for me to phone."

He didn't understand why. Then as he looked at the empty hooks, he reflected that, if he were away several days, customers would doubtless come to get their watches. There was nothing he could do about that. They would just have to understand.

"What time did you say, miss? . . . Six-seventeen? . . . Will you book a seat for Musak? . . . Frank Musak."

Now Dave knew why his friend had insisted upon telephoning: it was to spare him another assault by reporters and photographers at the airport.

"Thank you . . . no . . . one way. . . ."

Musak did not consult him. A little later he found himself outside with him. The moon had risen. Low clouds, dark at the center and brilliant at the edges, were gliding as though on calm water. For two or three minutes they remained there without speaking, standing on the sidewalk, where the rain had dried in patches, listening to the silence.

"We might as well go and get my car now."

He understood that too. Dave didn't have his car, which the police had kept. Musak intended to drive him to La Guardia. He did not protest and the two started to walk along Main Street, where there wasn't a soul. There were no lights to be seen except in the Old Barn Tavern, where two of the newspapermen were spending the night.

When they turned into the street, the grass, after the rain, smelled good.

"I'll get the car out," said Musak, going toward his garage.

Ben, too, must have relaxed, out there. If only they would let him sleep! He had always needed a lot of sleep and, in the morning, when his father woke him, it took him a long time to shake off his drowsiness; it even happened sometimes that, as he went, barefooted, in his pajamas to the bathroom, he bumped against the doorpost because he had not yet got his eyes properly open.

That was the time when he was grumpy. Only after his bath,

and even more after he had begun his breakfast, did he regain his normal spirits.

For the first time Galloway got into Musak's car and he found in it the same odor as in the carpenter's house.

"It's less than two hours from here to La Guardia. Allowing half an hour for you to get ready and have something to eat, that gives you nearly three hours' sleep."

He nearly protested; but his lids were drooping and it cost him an effort to hold his head upright. He could easily have fallen asleep in the car.

He wondered whether Musak intended, for his part, to sleep in Ben's bed. This would have shocked him. But Musak, back in the apartment, gave no sign of undressing, but settled down on the sofa as though for the rest of the night.

Dave went and undressed, was a little embarrassed at showing himself in pajamas.

"You'll wake me not later than quarter-past three?"

"Make it half-past," said Musak, setting the alarm as a precaution. "Go to sleep."

Two minutes later Dave had sunk deeply into slumber, but he could have sworn that he was conscious all the time of the presence of his friend, who had picked up a book and was smoking his pipe while he drank rye. Nor did he lose sight of the fact that he had to catch the plane at La Guardia at six-seventeen, or that the ticket was in Musak's name. Two or three times he turned over in a lump, as though to bury himself more deeply in the mattress, and when he again felt a touch on his shoulder, he sat up instantly. He had not heard the alarm. The apartment smelled of fresh coffee.

"Go have your bath."

He had never got up at this hour except when Ben was ill, one time, in particular, when he had a bad cold and had to be given medicine every two hours. On one occasion, during the latter half of the night, he had looked at his father with a frightened air and cried:

"What do you want?"

"It's time for your pill, Ben."

Did he hear? Did he understand? Frowning, his face screwed up, he continued to stare at his father as though he were seeing him for the first time and his eyes were hard.

"Can't you let me alone?" he said in a voice made husky by fever.

Dave had thought he sensed a resentment. Ben had taken his pill, drunk a mouthful of water, fallen asleep again, and in the morning, when his father referred to the episode, seemed not to remember it. But Galloway had never been quite sure that his son had not been in possession of his faculties at that moment. He avoided thinking about it. There had been three or four incidents like that in their life, and he preferred to forget them.

He was too susceptible, paid too much attention to Ben's least reactions. All children, like grownups, have moments of bad humor, even of instinctive rancor.

The smell of bacon reached him in the bathroom and it was that of the apartment on other mornings. He shaved carefully, chose his best clothes, as though this were of importance. Ben liked him to be well dressed. When they had first come to live in Everton and Dave had worn iron-gray smocks to work in, instead of the un-bleached smocks he later adopted, his son had once said to him:

"You look like a sick old man."

It was perhaps on this subject that he was most sensitive. He could not resign himself to appearing old in his son's eyes. In his presence he was less cordial with the customers, for fear of seeming obsequious.

"Feeling rested?"

"You've gone to a lot of trouble," he said, looking at the table, the eggs and bacon on a big dish, the toast in the electric toaster.

He knew it had been a pleasure to Musak, just as it was for him to do all the things he used to do for his son.

Around them an absolute calm prevailed in the town, and when they started the car they were almost ashamed of the noise they set up.

"Have you been to Indianapolis before?" asked Musak as they reached the highway.

"Never."

"I have."

He said nothing more, allowed his companion to sleep, keeping in his mouth his unlit pipe, on which he drew mechanically, and it made its familiar sound. At the airport they had nearly half an hour to wait. On the newspaper stands headlines announced:

"Sixteen-year-old killer."

For, because of Sunday, the papers had not yet been able to report the events of the previous night. Galloway frowned as he caught sight of his son's photograph, which he scarcely recognized. He didn't remember that photograph. Ben seemed younger, with a curious, vague stare and a sort of smirk at the corners of his mouth. He had to look at it more closely to see that the head had been cut out of a group taken at high school. One of Ben's friends, no doubt, had given the newspapermen a copy.

There was also a photograph of Lillian, in which she did not look more than twelve years old.

A subhead said:

"Twenty-four-hour man hunt ends in shooting on Indiana farm."

He bought three different papers while Musak watched him without saying a word, looking displeased. On one page his own photograph was displayed, standing in front of Ben's bed, of which one only saw a part, and another in which he was pretending to work on a watch in his shop.

Everything here was gray and gloomy. People were sleeping on the benches. Those who had their eyes open stared in front of them with a depressed air. A couple embraced, the woman was crying, clinging to her companion as though they were separating for life.

His plane was announced. He went toward the doorway indicated by the loud-speaker and no one seemed to take any notice of him. An official called out the names of the passengers.

"Musak," he murmured as he passed.

He had shaken the cabinetmaker's hand, saying simply:

"Thanks. Now, everything will be all right."

He was convinced of it. He did not look at the papers until after they had loosened their safety belts and he turned at once to the last paragraphs, those dealing with events on the farm:

"While the Illinois state police were keeping watch for the fugitives at all the crossroads, the latter turned back and again drove into Indiana. Was Ben Galloway at the end of his strength, after spending twenty-three hours at the wheel, or was he afraid to run the risk of filling his tank? In any case a little later the car stopped at an isolated farm, twenty miles from the border.

"It was about ten at night. The farmer, Hans Putman, aged fifty, was still up, as was his wife, and both were in a room on the ground floor.

"When Putman answered the knocks at the door, he found himself facing Galloway, who leveled his automatic at him and told the girl:

" 'Cut the telephone line.'

"He seemed exhausted. His hands were trembling with fatigue.

" 'Get us something to eat and don't anyone try to leave the house.'

"By that time, the Putman boy, who had been upstairs when the car arrived, had slipped out by a back way and was bicycling to the nearest house, so that ten minutes later the sheriff was notified and in a little while three police cars were converging on the farm."

Other passengers were reading the same story as himself and had seen his photograph, but no one seemed to recognize him.

"With the house surrounded, the sheriff and one of his men went toward the door and what happened then is still not very clear. Galloway and his companion certainly tried to escape by way of the farmyard. The inquiry will establish who was the first to shoot. A burst of shots was fired and one of the policemen was hit by a bullet in the hip.

"In the end the young man shouted, using his hands as a megaphone:

" 'Don't shoot any more, I surrender.'

"His automatic was empty.

"While he was being taken to Jasonville, where he was to be handed over to FBI agents who were to take him to Indianapolis, he expressed no regret for his actions.

" 'If it hadn't been for a boy my age, you wouldn't have caught me,' he said, referring to the Putman boy, who is also apparently sixteen years old.

"He ended by falling asleep in the car while his companion kept her eyes wide open as though to watch over him."

It was probably not wholly true, because it is impossible to report the words and deeds of anyone with entire accuracy. Ben's words, however, must surely be authentic:

"If it hadn't been for a boy my age . . ."

And also, perhaps, the fact that Lillian Hawkins had kept awake during the journey to watch over him. This detail disturbed Galloway, made him sullen. It seemed to him, without his being able to explain why, that because of her, things were going to be less simple than he had thought.

He dozed, a lighter sleep than in the apartment, broken into by three or four awakenings. Once he saw a woman with a baby in her arms gazing intently at him. A newspaper lay open on the seat beside her. She must have recognized him. When he met her gaze and glanced mechanically at the child, she shuddered, as though she were mentally making heaven knew what comparison, and clasped the baby more tightly to her.

When he had been left alone with him, Ben had been scarcely older than that baby. Galloway had not suffered, in reality, from his wife's departure. One would have said that he had always expected it. Who knows? After the first shock it was perhaps a relief to him that she had vanished from their life.

He did not like remembering Ruth, or that time. Until he was twenty-five the idea of marriage had never occurred to him and he associated with women only to the extent that was necessary: he was over twenty before he first had sexual relations with a woman.

At Waterbury, Ruth worked in the same shop as he. He knew she went out every evening with one man or another and haunted the bars, where, after a couple of drinks, she became vulgar and noisy.

She was not yet twenty, but she had left her parents' farm, in Ohio, when she was scarcely sixteen and had lived in New York, in Albany, perhaps in still other places before landing in Waterbury.

She worried neither about tomorrow nor about what people thought of her. For months he had watched her, convinced that she had a sort of contempt for him, because he did not amuse himself like the others. She attracted and frightened him both at once. She was a female rather than a woman and the very movement of her hips sufficed to disturb him.

One evening as he came out of the workshop and was about to go toward the streetcar, he found her standing motionless beside him on the sidewalk.

He never knew if she had been waiting for him.

"Do I scare you?" she asked him as he looked at her with embarrassment.

He said no. She had a hoarse voice, stood very close to men she talked to.

"Are you waiting for someone?"

She laughed, as though he had said something comic, and, blushing, he had been on the point of going away. Even now he did not know what had held him back.

"What's so funny about me?"

"The way you look at me."

"Shall we have dinner together?"

He had been wanting to, in reality, for a long time, but until then had never thought it possible. Throughout the evening he was embarrassed by the way she behaved, first in the restaurant, then in the two or three bars where she led him and where, at the end, she had drunk neat whisky.

He could have spent the night with her. She had been surprised when he had left her at her door. All next day, in the workshop, she had watched him as though she were trying to understand, and his manner had been cold toward her.

For a week he had said practically not a word to her, but one night after he had seen her getting into a friend's car it had taken him at least two hours to get to sleep. The next day he had asked her:

"Are you free this evening?"

"My! Has it come over you again?"

He had looked at her in such a way that she had been sobered.

"If you really want to, wait for me outside."

They had followed the same program as the first time. His manner had been somber and he had deliberately drunk more than usual. At the moment of taking leave of her, on her doorstep, he had said as he looked at her in the same hard, hostile fashion as that morning:

"Will you marry me?"

"Me?"

She laughed, then laughed no more, studied him more attentively, and her face betrayed both astonishment and a certain unease.

"What's gotten into you? Is it the whisky?"

"You know very well it isn't."

And it was true that she knew it.

"We'll talk about it some other time," she murmured, turning toward the door.

He had grasped her wrist.

"No. Tonight."

She had not asked him in. She was genuinely frightened of him.

"Let's walk!"

For nearly two hours they had walked up and down the pavement, between the same two lampposts, and they had not held each other by the arm, not stopped to embrace.

"Why do you want to marry me?"

His forehead stubborn, he replied:

"Because!"

"And if you could have what you want in any case?"

"I'd still marry you."

"You aren't the sort of man to live with a woman like me."

Why was she the one he suddenly thought of, in his half sleep, after just seeing a child in its mother's arms? For years he had repulsed that memory.

"Do you reckon you'll be happy with me?"

He hadn't answered. It wasn't a question of happiness. He could not have explained himself, and in any case it was too turbulent to be expressed. What mattered was that he had made his decision and was sticking to it.

"Is it yes?"

"I'll give you my answer tomorrow."

"No. Right now."

He had married her two weeks later, without having previously had relations with her, and the next day had forbidden her to go to work.

She was Ben's mother. She had left him one night, twenty months later, without being tempted to take the child with her. He had not been angered by her going. What he had felt that first night in the empty house was chagrin, as though he had suffered a setback. He knew what he meant by this. This setback was one he was bound to encounter sooner or later, because it went back a very long way, to things that had existed in him when he was still a child.

It was nobody's business. He had to forget it. Ben remained with him and that alone mattered.

Someday, much later on, when Ben would be quite a man, they might perhaps talk it over together and Dave would tell him the truth.

The notion that perhaps there would never be a "later on," that his son would not be given time to become a man, had never entered his head and, at Indianapolis, he nearly rushed straight to the Police Court without stopping to leave his suitcase at the hotel. He changed his mind on the way, in the taxi.

"Drop me first at a hotel," he said.

"In the center of town?"

"As near the Police Court as possible."

Now that he was so near his son, he was overtaken by feverishness. He saw a huge square surrounded by stone buildings, recognized what must be the Capitol, then, farther off, the post office with capitals supported by white columns.

The driver thrust down his flag outside a hotel that looked luxurious.

"I'd like you to wait for me."

"The Police Court's right there," the man replied, pointing to a building.

He passed through a revolving door behind a porter who carried his suitcase and led him to the desk.

"Did you make a reservation?"

"No. I'd like a room."

A pad of forms was handed to him and he wrote his real name, which the clerk read upside down. Perhaps because he knew at once why he had come, he did not ask how many days he expected to be staying.

"Show Mr. Galloway up to 662."

He had not wanted to go up to his room, but did not venture to protest. Being there, he took advantage of the fact to wash his hands and face and comb his hair.

He hoped they had not started interrogating Ben immediately and had let him sleep. Had they allowed him to wash and change his clothes?

When he crossed the lobby, several people followed him with their eyes.

This no longer had any effect on him; he felt no self-consciousness.

It was ten in the morning. At the Police Court lawyers, judges, messengers were going from one door to another, preoccupied, with dossiers in their hands, and, feeling suddenly lost, he turned for help to the uniformed attendant standing by the door.

"Do you know if Ben Galloway is in the building?" he asked.

"Who?"

"Ben Galloway. The one who——"

"Oh! Sure."

The man looked at him more closely. He must have seen his picture in the paper.

"He isn't here," he went on in an altered voice. "I know there was a conference, this morning, in the District Attorney's office. The newspapermen have been here three or four times already. If you want my opinion, you're most likely to find him at the FBI office."

"Where are they?"

"In the Federal Building, over the post office. You know where the post office is?"

"I saw it as I came here."

People stopped to look at him. One man, he thought, was about to come up and speak to him, changed his mind at the last moment. It was probably an official, perhaps one of the District Attorney's assistants, or perhaps a lawyer wanting to offer his services.

The sun was brilliant, the day already hot, women were wearing light-colored dresses and many of the men already had on their Panama hats. He was walking quickly. In a few minutes he would know, perhaps would be face to face with Ben.

The Federal Building was bright, with wide marble-paved corridors, mahogany doors, each bearing a brass number. He knocked on the one that had been pointed out to him. A voice called to him to come in and a middle-aged woman, with gray hair, for a moment stopped typing.

"What can I do for you?"

"I want to see my son. I'm Dave Galloway, Ben's father."

It was not the sentence he had prepared. He was wasting no

words, looking at a half-open door on his left, at another, on his
right, which was shut.

"Please sit down."

"Can you tell me if my son's here?"

Without answering she picked up the telephone and said:

"Mr. Dave Galloway's in the anteroom."

She sat listening, punctuating the utterances of the person at
the other end with:

"Yes . . . Yes . . . Very well . . . I understand . . ."

He had obeyed mechanically when she asked him to be seated,
but he was already on his feet again.

"I'm going to see him?" he asked.

"He is busy right now. He'll see you in a little while."

"You aren't allowed to tell me if my son's here, straight out?"

Embarrassed, she murmured as she started typing again:

"I've had no instructions."

The Venetian blinds, lowered, let through evenly spaced bars
of light, which were reflected on the walls and the ceiling. A fan
was turning almost soundlessly.

Resigned to remaining seated, his hat on his knees, he followed
with his eyes the carriage of the typewriter, then the movement of
the second hand on the electric clock built into one of the parti-
tions.

A youngish man came out of the office on the left, papers in
hand, glanced at him, frowned, examined him again more closely
while he was pulling open the metal drawers of a filing cabinet.
When he had found what he wanted and made some notes on a
document, he leaned over the secretary and spoke to her in a low
voice.

It was something to do with Galloway. But neither of them ad-
dressed him and the man disappeared through the door by which
he had come.

Dave was attentive to every sound. Apart from the tapping of
the machine, he could hear nothing but footsteps in the big corridor, now and then knocks on a door. The telephone rang, the
woman answered:

"Just a minute, please. Hold on."

She pushed buttons.

"Albany's on the line."

He nearly rose to his feet again. Albany—that must certainly be something to do with Ben. While he was waiting, powerless, in an anteroom, it was his son's fate that they were discussing!

This was something he had not foreseen, this impossibility, not merely of seeing Ben immediately upon his arrival, but of talking to someone, no matter whom, someone who could tell him what was happening.

A half hour went by, the longest, most painful of his life. Twice more the telephone rang, messages were passed to the mysterious inspector who lurked in one of the offices, hidden from sight. Once the woman simply announced:

"The Governor."

He could understand at a pinch that they would not be able to receive him immediately. At least they could have told him whether Ben was here. He was his father. He had a right to see him, to speak to him.

"Listen, miss . . ."

"Be patient, Mr. Galloway. It won't be much longer."

She knew what was happening herself! He tried to glean something from her expression, but she paid no attention to him, continued to type with a dizzy rapidity.

At one moment a door opened in the corridor nearby, perhaps the one next to them, and, if he had obeyed his instinct, he would have darted out to look. He dared not, too subdued, fearing a rebuke from the gray-haired lady. Almost immediately afterward the right-hand door, the one that had hitherto remained closed, opened in its turn, a man about his own age stood in the doorway, looked toward him.

"Will you come in, Mr. Galloway?"

There were the same Venetian blinds over the windows, the same reflections quivering on the light-colored walls. The man pointed to a chair, sat down himself behind a huge metal desk on which, in a frame, Dave noticed the photograph of a woman and two children.

He opened his mouth to ask the question to which he was at length to receive a reply, when the other spoke first, in a quiet voice, a little cold, in which however he thought he could discern some sympathy or pity.

"I suppose you got here on the first plane?"

"Yes. I——"

"You know, you shouldn't have left before hearing from us. Unfortunately you've made the trip for nothing."

He felt his limbs grow cold.

"My son isn't here?"

"He's to be taken to New York, and from there to Freedom, New York, all in the course of today."

Dave didn't understand, stared at the other man as he tried to do so.

"The murder at the start, which was committed in New York State, is more important than the assaults that took place here. The question was whether your son was first to be tried in Indiana for having fired at the police and wounding an officer, or whether he should go for trial right away in New York State. The governors of the two states got in touch by phone this morning and came to an agreement."

"He hasn't already gone?" he protested.

The man glanced at a clock exactly like the one there was in the anteroom.

"No. Right now, they're probably having a meal."

"Where?"

"I'm sorry I can't tell you, Mr. Galloway. In order to avoid all unnecessary publicity and possible incidents, we have arranged matters so that even the newspapermen don't know they spent the night here and they're waiting for them at the door of the prison."

"Ben was *here?*"

With his finger he indicated the room in which they were seated and the other nodded.

"He was in here when I arrived, wasn't he?"

The man nodded again.

"And I was made to wait, deliberately, in the anteroom, so that I wouldn't see him?" he cried finally, unable to control himself any longer.

"Take it easy, Mr. Galloway. It wasn't I who prevented you from meeting your son."

"Who was it?"

"It was he who refused to see you."

7

I'm afraid, Mr. Galloway, that all of us, without exception, are the last people to know our own children."

The man, at that moment, was filling his pipe with slow, careful movements and, as though to emphasize the fact that he did not except himself, he allowed his gaze to rest for a moment on the photograph on his desk.

Dave uttered no protest, because all his life he had had an instinctive respect for everything that represented authority. What the man had just said, in any case, was probably true for certain fathers, for ordinary fathers, but it was not for him.

What good would it do to try and explain their life, Ben's life and his, the nature of their relationship, which was not merely the relationship of father and son?

"I don't know," the FBI man went on, leaning back in his chair, "what they will decide about him. Our part, here, is over. I imagine his lawyer, if not the District Attorney himself, will insist on his being examined by one or more psychiatrists."

Galloway almost smiled, so absurd did it seem to him to suppose that Ben was not in full possession of his reason. If he was not normal, then his father was not normal either. But Dave could not have reached the age of forty-three without the fact being apparent.

"I had him here from midnight until a few minutes ago and I must confess I haven't been able to make up my mind about him."

"Ben's not easy to get to know," his father hastened to say.

The other man seemed surprised.

"Well, at least," he retorted, "he showed no sign of shyness, if that's what you mean. I've seldom seen anyone at any age so much at ease in similar circumstances. They were brought into my office together, he and his girl friend, and you'd have thought they were delighted to be here, as though in spite of everything they'd done what they set out to do. When the handcuffs were taken off them, they drew close to one another and held hands.

"It didn't matter that they were dirty and tired, their eyes were clear. They took pleasure in looking at one another with a sort of jubilation, as though they shared a marvelous secret.

"I said to them:

" 'You can sit down.'

"And your son said coolly:

" 'We've had enough sitting down on the trip.'

"He was watching me, ironically, I could swear.

" 'Is this where you give us the third degree?' he shot at me with a smile that was just a little nervous all the same. 'If you want confessions, I confess everything, the murder of the old boy on the highway, the theft of the car, the threats to the farmer and his wife, and the shots fired at the police. I'm not accused of anything else, am I?'

" 'There's no question of interrogating you at present,' I said. 'You're almost asleep on your feet.'

"That seemed to upset him, as though I weren't playing the game according to the rules.

" 'I can still last out the night if I have to. As far as Lillian's concerned, you can let her go. She hasn't done anything. She didn't know my plans. I just told her we were going to Illinois or Mississippi to get married and she didn't know I was armed.'

"The girl interrupted him.

" 'That's not true!'

" 'You've got to believe me. When we left the farm, she begged me to give myself up without shooting.'

" 'He's lying. What we did, we did together. The justice of the peace in Illinois didn't marry us, but since last night I've been his wife just the same.' "

Galloway had withdrawn into himself and now nothing of his feelings showed.

"I thought they were going to start an argument between themselves and I sent them to bed. Your son slept on a camp bed in the next room and Lillian Hawkins spent the night in another office in charge of a policewoman.

"The girl slept restlessly. As for the boy, he slept as though he were in his own bed and they had some trouble waking him."

"He has always been a heavy sleeper."

"It's true that I had no intention of putting him through a proper interrogation, because that's the business of the District Attorney, in Freedom, the seat of the county where the crime was committed. It's only about fifty miles from your home, if I'm not mistaken. Do you know anyone in Freedom, Mr. Galloway?"

"No one."

"That's where your son and his girl will be tried if the psychiatrists decide that they should go for trial. This morning, I had coffee and rolls sent up to them and they both had good appetites. While I was putting through some phone calls, I watched them. They were sitting just there . . ."

He pointed to a dark leather sofa against the wall.

". . . they were holding hands, like last night, whispering, gazing ecstatically into each other's eyes. Anyone not knowing the facts who had come in at that moment would have taken them for the happiest pair on earth. When I was notified of your arrival, I said to your son:

" 'Your father's here.'

"I don't want to cause you pain, Mr. Galloway, but I think it's important you should know the truth. He turned toward his girl, scowling, and he muttered between his teeth:

" 'Hell!'

"I went on:

" 'I can allow you to see him for a few minutes, alone if you like.'

" 'But I don't want to see him at all!' he cried. 'I've nothing to say to him. Do you have to let him come in?'

" 'I can't compel you to see him.'

" 'Well, then, it's no!'

"Other people will be handling the rest of the business and I confess to you that, personally, I'd rather not have to come to a decision where he's concerned."

"He's not mad," Dave repeated with conviction.

"Just the same that's his only chance. I wonder if you realize it. Now if you'll promise me to do nothing that might cause an incident, if you think you're capable of seeing your son pass close by you without rushing toward him . . ."

"I promise."

"I'll give you a piece of information that is still confidential. At twelve forty-five, your son and Lillian Hawkins will arrive at the airport, with police officers, to catch the New York plane. They'll

just go through the hall where there will certainly be a few reporters and one or two photographers. If you happen to be there . . ."

"They're traveling in an ordinary plane?"

The inspector nodded.

"I'm entitled to catch the same one?"

"If there's room."

He had an hour and a half to spare, but he was so afraid of being late that he hurriedly left the Federal Building and ran to his
hotel.

"I have to leave by the twelve-forty-five plane," he said. "I've
come to get my suitcase. How much do I owe you?" ·

"Nothing, Mr. Galloway, since you haven't used the room."

He returned in a taxi along that morning's route, ran instantly
to the ticket office.

"Is there any room left in the twelve-forty-five plane for New
York?"

"How many seats?"

"Only one."

"Just a minute."

It was very hot. The girl had beads of sweat on her upper lip,
damp circles under her arms, and her odor recalled that of Ruth.
She telephoned another office.

"What name?" she then asked, preparing to fill in a ticket.

"Galloway."

She looked at him, astonished, hesitated.

"Do you know that in the same plane . . ."

"My son will be there, yes."

He had lunch at the airport restaurant. What the FBI man had
told him did not yet trouble him, perhaps because he was still living on his built-up momentum. Only when he had been told about
Lillian, and what she had proudly proclaimed on the subject of
their relationship, had he felt a tightening at his heart.

If Ben had refused to see him, it was obviously because he was
embarrassed at the thought of being confronted by him. He, too,
was in a nervous state. He must be allowed time to recover.

At a quarter-past twelve, already, Galloway was at the entrance
to the airport, watching the cars arrive, and he had asked two different attendants if they were sure there was no other way in. He
saw some photographers arrive with their cameras and the three

men who joined them were no doubt reporters. They formed a group in the middle of the hall and one of them caught sight of him, wrinkled his forehead, spoke to the others, went and questioned the girl in the ticket office, who nodded.

He had been recognized. He didn't care. They all came up to him together.

"Mr. Galloway?"

He said yes.

"Did you see your son this morning?"

He was on the verge of lying, so much did it cost him to have to admit that he had made the journey for nothing.

"I wasn't able to see him."

"Were you refused permission?"

He was tempted to say yes, but his reply would appear in the papers and the FBI man would probably contradict it.

"It was my son who didn't want to see me," he confessed, forcing a smile as though he were talking of a piece of boyish naughtiness. "You should be able to understand his reaction. . . ."

"You're going to make the trip with him?"

"In the same plane, yes."

"The trial will be held in Freedom?"

"That's what I was told an hour ago."

"Have you chosen a lawyer?"

"No. I'll get the best; I can afford it."

He was ashamed of himself, suddenly, realizing that he was behaving ridiculously.

"Do you mind?" he was asked. "Take a step forward. Thanks."

He was photographed. And it was at this moment that he saw his son getting out of a car, his wrist linked by a handcuff to the wrist of a police officer in plain clothes who was young and looked like his elder brother. Ben was wearing his fawn-colored raincoat. He was bareheaded; Lillian Hawkins was following him, accompanied by a plump woman, tightly enclosed in a dark suit that made one think of a uniform.

Two big bay windows were open. Had Ben recognized his father, at a distance, under the photographers' flashes? The newspapermen made a rush for the doorway, and the crowd, which quickly grasped what was happening, was already beginning to form itself into a hedge, as though for the passing of an official personage.

Dave was using his elbows, working his way into the front row and, when his son was only a few yards from the inner door, their eyes met, Ben frowned and went straight on, turned a little later, not to look at him again, but to say something to Lillian.

She was a little more pale than he, no doubt from fatigue, and in her cheap coat covering a flowered cotton dress she looked, beside the policewoman, like a little ailing child.

Ben had made no movement toward his father and Dave began to understand, now, what the FBI man had tried to tell him. It was as though sixteen years of shared life and daily intimacy had suddenly ceased to exist. There had been no glint in his son's eyes, no emotion on his face. Nothing but a knitting of his brows, as when one sees something unpleasing in one's way.

"My father!" he must have said to the girl as he turned to her.

They had already vanished onto the airfield, where they were to board the plane before the barrier was opened for the other passengers.

"Did he see you?" one of the reporters asked him.

"I think so."

He added:

"I'm not sure."

He followed the queue, was one of the last to enter the plane, where the stewardess showed him to one of the back seats. Ben and Lillian, on the other hand, were right in front, he on the left with the policeman, she on the right with the woman escorting her, and there was only the aisle between them.

By rising in his seat Dave could catch sight of them. He could see nothing but their heads and the backs of their necks, and this only when they were not leaning back, but it was enough for him to realize that they were turned toward one another the whole time. They sometimes leaned sideways and exchanged remarks and their escorts did not interfere. A little later the stewardesses offered them sandwiches, as she did the other passengers, and they refused.

Was it possible that neither of them realized their position? One might have thought they were on vacation, happy to be making a trip by plane, and Dave saw that the other passengers were as astonished at their behavior as himself.

After about half an hour in the air Lillian's head slipped gradually sideways and she must have slept nearly all the rest of the journey. As for Ben, after chatting for a time in a low voice with the policeman, he read the paper the man offered him.

All this was nothing but a misunderstanding; Galloway was sure of it. The actions of others always appear strange to us because we do not know their true motives. When he had married Ruth, way back, everyone in the workshop had regarded him with a mingled astonishment and commiseration and he had turned to them very much the same face that Ben turned to the crowd.

He knew what he was doing when he married Ruth. He had been the only one to know.

People were sorry for him. They imagined he had let himself be bewitched, that he had yielded to a passing infatuation, not realizing that she was the only kind of woman he could have any desire to marry. Who knows? Perhaps some of them had thought that he had temporarily gone out of his mind?

He too had held his wife's hand in public, gazing defiantly at the world. And, when she was pregnant, he had walked proudly beside her through the center of town.

Most of his friends had had her. In spite of this he hadn't permitted himself to touch her before their marriage, and this, strangely, had so moved her that she had wept as she thanked him. It was true that they had been drinking that night. They drank every night.

Everyone would have predicted that he would be unhappy with her and it had not been the case at all. He had insisted upon living in one of the new houses on the development, like most young couples, on buying the same furniture, the same knickknacks. His mother had not been present at the wedding because he had only told her about it a month later, casually, at the end of a letter, as though it were news of no importance. The following spring she had paid them an unexpected visit with Musselman and he was sure she had never been so surprised in her life. He didn't know what she had expected; it certainly wasn't Ruth, or the little household her eyes beheld.

"Are you happy?" she had asked him when for a moment they were alone together.

He was content to smile and she didn't believe his smile. She'd never believed him. She'd never believed his father, either. Did she believe Musselman?

"Well, children, it's time for us to be going!"

She had not accepted their invitation to dinner.

"Good luck!" she had called, once on the sidewalk.

She wished the pair of them every conceivable disaster. So he had not written when Ruth left him. He had gone nearly two years without answering her letters, which were in any case not frequent.

Was this what the FBI man had tried to make him understand that morning? The difference lay, precisely, in the fact that he trusted Ben. They were of the same breed. He was truly his son. Tonight, tomorrow, they would have a talk and everything would be explained. What Ben had to know was that his father already understood. It was implied in his message:

"I'll always be on your side, no matter what happens. . . ."

He had added, to emphasize it still more:

"I'm not angry with you. . . ."

It was not a matter of being angry in the strict sense of the word. It was bigger than that. Ben had probably not heard his radio message since, at about the time when it was broadcast, he had been calling on the justice of the peace in a village in Illinois.

Was he the one who, later that evening, had stopped the car in the darkness, regardless of the police on their trail, and proposed to Lillian that they should belong to one another? Had it been her idea? He preferred not to think about that, or to try to guess what they were saying now that the girl had just waked up.

They were flying over New York, whose skyscrapers could be seen almost golden in the sunshine, and the plane was steadily losing altitude. They had put out cigarettes, buckled their safety belts. Dave had intended to stay in his seat until his son went out, so that he would be obliged to pass very close to him and even brush against him, but the stewardess made all the passengers go first, himself included.

He was obliged to follow the others through the gate and, when he reached the waiting room and looked around, he saw that Ben and Lillian were being taken to another part of the airfield.

"Where are they going?" he asked an attendant.

The man looked in the direction to which he was pointing.

"Most likely to catch another plane," he said indifferently.

"What line is that, down there?"

"Syracuse."

"Does the plane land at Freedom?"

"Probably."

He tried in vain to catch it. By the time he had found the right ticket window, the plane had already taken off.

"There's another flight in an hour's time that stops at Freedom. You'll still get there faster than by train."

He no longer let himself grow impatient, was beginning to get used to the fact that everything turned out differently from what he hoped, and he did not lose courage, being convinced that it was he who would have the last word.

It was five o'clock when he reached the county capital, which he had only driven through by car before. The last time was the previous day, in a police car, and everything was shut because it was Sunday. He took just time to leave his suitcase at the hotel, without going up to his room, this time, and hurried to the Police Court, which was not far off.

He arrived there a few minutes too late. A group of sight-seers and a photographer were still standing on the stone steps.

"Is Ben Galloway in the building?" he asked.

"He's just been taken away."

"Where?"

"To the County Jail."

"Has he seen the District Attorney?"

"They were both taken to his office, but they only stayed a few minutes."

He had not been recognized. He tried to push through the glass-paned door and it wouldn't open. From inside a doorkeeper with a chevroned cap, who had lost an arm, motioned to him to stop.

"He won't open it," said an old man. "At five sharp they shut the doors and then no one's allowed in."

"Is the District Attorney still in his office?"

"Probably. I haven't seen him come out. But he won't see you after hours either."

The old man, whose denture did not fit very well, regarded him with a sly smile.

"You're the father, aren't you?"

And, as Galloway nodded, he added in a shrill voice:

"A fine son you've got there! Something to be proud of!"

It was the first gratuitous insult he had suffered because of Ben and, taken aback, not understanding, he stared after the little old man as he went off chuckling.

He had gone about it the wrong way, from the start. He should have listened to the lieutenant, who had advised him to engage a good lawyer immediately. What did he know about the formalities with which one had to comply in order to visit a prisoner? He undoubtedly had rights, but he did not know what they were. Ben had to be protected. He must not be allowed to go on talking and acting like a child.

He went back to the hotel, not knowing where else to turn.

"Could I see the manager?"

Without being kept waiting he was shown into a small office near the reception desk. The manager was jacketless, his shirt sleeves rolled up.

"Sid Nicholson," he introduced himself.

"Dave Galloway. I suppose you know why I'm here?"

"Yes, I know, Mr. Galloway."

"I want to ask you if you can tell me the best lawyer in the county."

He added with unnecessary bravado:

"Never mind if he's expensive. I can pay."

"You should try to get Wilbur Lane."

"Is he the best?"

"He's not only the best in Freedom, but he has cases pretty well every week in New York and Albany and he's a personal friend of the Governor. Do you want to see him tonight?"

"If possible."

"In that case, I'd better call him up right away, because when he leaves his office it'll be to go to the golf course, and you won't have another chance."

"I'd be glad if you would."

"Get me Wilbur Lane, Jane."

There was a secretary at the other end of the line whom he also called by her Christian name.

"Is the boss still there? Sid Nicholson. I'd like to have a word with him. It's urgent. . . . Hello, Wilbur? Sorry to disturb you.

You were just getting ready to leave? . . . I have someone here who wants your help . . . Can't you guess? . . . That's who it is. He's in my office . . . You can see him? . . . I'll send him right over . . . So long . . ."

"Where is it?" asked Galloway, who had heard.

"You go down the street till you see a little Methodist chapel, on your right. Exactly opposite, there's a big, white, colonial-style house with the names 'Lane, Pepper, and Durkin' on the name plate. Jed Pepper handles only taxation and wills. As for Durkin, he died six months ago."

The offices had been closed since five o'clock, but the secretary must have been keeping watch for him at one of the windows, because she opened the door the moment he set foot on the flight of steps.

"Mr. Lane's waiting for you. This way, please."

A white-haired man, his face still youthful, who stood a head taller than Galloway and had the build of a football player, stood up to shake hands with him.

"I won't go so far as to say I was expecting you, which would be fatuous on my part, but I wasn't surprised when my friend Sid called me up. Sit down, Mr. Galloway. I've been reading in the afternoon paper that you made a fruitless trip to Indianapolis."

"My son's here."

"I know. I've just this minute contacted George Temple, the District Attorney, who's an old friend. He, too, understood at once what it was about."

"I want you to undertake my son's defense. I'm not rich, but I have about seven thousand dollars saved and———"

"We'll talk about that later. Whom did you see, in Indianapolis?"

"A man who seemed to be head of the FBI there. They didn't tell me his name."

"What did you say to him?"

"That I was convinced everything would be explained when I'd had a talk with Ben."

"And your son refused to see you."

Noting Galloway's surprise, he explained:

"It's in the papers already. You must understand, it's important, from now on, that you avoid talking about this business to anyone at all and especially to newspapermen. Even if they ask you questions about your son that seem quite harmless, don't answer. Temple didn't want to take advantage of the situation and interrogate the pair as soon as they left the plane. So they only spent a few minutes at his office for the usual formalities and he sent them straight to the jail. Tomorrow, since you want me to undertake your son's defense, I will be present when he undergoes his first interrogation. Probably I shall have a chance to talk to him even before then."

He asked bluntly, while thrusting a cigar into a holder with a gold band:

"What's he like?"

Dave flushed, because he did not understand the exact sense of the question and was afraid of going wrong again.

"He's always been a quiet, thoughtful boy," he said. "In sixteen years, he has never once given me any trouble."

"What was he like when you saw him in Indianapolis? According to the papers you came face to face at the airport."

"Not quite face to face. I was in the crowd."

"He saw you?"

"Yes."

"He seemed embarrassed?"

"No. It's hard to explain. I suppose he was annoyed at finding me there."

"Is his mother still alive?"

"I imagine so."

"You don't know where she is?"

"She left me fifteen and a half years ago, leaving me the child, who was then six months old. Three years later, someone brought me some papers to sign so she could get a divorce."

"Any weaknesses on that side?"

"What do you mean?"

"I'm asking you whether his antecedents, on his mother's side, might explain what has happened."

"To my knowledge, she has never been sick."

"And you?"

He had not expected questions of this sort and was nonplussed by them, the more so since the lawyer was writing down his replies. His hands were carefully tended, his nails manicured. He was dressed in a double-breasted blue suit, admirably cut. For some moments Dave had been wondering whom he reminded him of.

"I've never had any serious illness either."

"Your father?"

"He died of a heart attack at the age of forty."

"Your mother?"

"She married again and is in good health."

"No aunts, uncles, cousins, male or female, who at any time had to be put in a mental home?"

He realized where these questions were heading, protested:

"Ben isn't mad!"

"Don't shout it so loud, because it may very well be our only chance of saving his skin. You know, when I read what the papers said about his attitude, I thought at first he was doing everything he could to get himself sent to the electric chair. I'm sorry to put it crudely. We have to look the facts in the face. Afterwards, thinking it over, I wondered, and I'm still wondering, whether he isn't more crafty than we think and if he hasn't adopted the best tactics."

"I don't understand."

"He doesn't cry, doesn't say he's sorry, doesn't collapse, doesn't shut himself up in a mistrustful silence, either. On the contrary, he talks and behaves as though he were delighted at having killed a man, in cold blood; at having stolen his car and having, later on, opened fire and gone on shooting until his automatic was empty.

"It is difficult, my dear sir, to conceive of an intelligent youth, who has attained his sixteenth year and has been normally raised in middle-class society, it is difficult, I say, to imagine him behaving in this way unless his mind is deranged.

"The word 'madness' frightens you, as it does everyone, and in any case it's not precise enough. The psychiatrists will use more exact terms in establishing first your son's degree of understanding, secondly his capacity for reacting to a good or evil impulse.

"This expert examination is the first thing I shall demand tomorrow of the District Attorney and it's more than probable that I shall call in a New York specialist."

Had Dave been going to persist in repeating that his son was not mad? He was not listened to. He was given to understand that this was no longer his business, that Ben's defense was no longer in his hands.

"I take it you intend to stay in Freedom until the case goes before the jury? Unless the expert examination I have just mentioned takes longer than I expect, the jury will be summoned in two or three days.

"I don't want to prevent you from staying, but it's preferable that you should show yourself as little as possible and above all that you should avoid saying anything. There's a telephone in every room in the hotel. I promise to keep you informed. If I think it desirable that you should have an interview with your son, I'll make arrangements with the District Attorney.

"While waiting, you can help me and occupy your mind by trying to remember every more or less unusual incident in the course of your son's life. Don't tell me there haven't been any. You'll be surprised how much you'll discover."

He glanced at his watch and stood up. Was he perhaps telling himself that there was still time for his game of golf? It was as they shook hands that Dave suddenly realized of whom he reminded him.

It was of Musselman, his mother's second husband.

It was too late to change his mind. Besides, Musselman was efficient at his job. This one was too, no doubt.

He was thrust into the background, he was told to keep quiet, almost to hide himself, and it was the lawyer who would decide whether or not an interview between father and son was desirable!

He walked along the street and people turned to look at him. When he pushed through the revolving door of the hotel, he saw, in a corner of the entrance hall, Isabel Hawkins, wearing her best dress and hat. She was talking to someone he did not immediately recognize because his back was turned.

It was Evan Cavanaugh, the Everton lawyer. They must have arrived together a short time previously. Dave had not once thought of the Hawkinses, still less that Lillian Hawkins would need a lawyer also. It gave him an odd feeling.

Isabel Hawkins had seen him. They both looked at each other. Instead of greeting him, of giving a sign of recognition, she pressed her lips together and her little eyes became hard.

He was almost gratified to learn that they were enemies.

8

Toward eleven, through his window, he saw Isabel Hawkins leave the hotel with Cavanaugh and go in the direction of the Police Court, and he could not help envying her. His own lawyer had not yet telephoned and, in the expectation of a call, Dave had not left his room for an instant.

He was still at the window, still without news, when Isabel came back, alone this time, after having spent three quarters of an hour at the court. Had she been with her daughter all this time? She only entered the hotel and came out again and, carrying her small suitcase, walked toward the bus depot.

She was going back to Everton. Perhaps he should telephone Musak, who had helped him as best he could to get through Sunday night and had driven him to La Guardia in his car.

What could he say to him? It seemed to him that an eternity had passed since then and he wondered if he would ever see Everton again.

Wilbur Lane called him a few minutes later. Did he really speak more coldly than the previous evening, or was that merely the impression his voice gave over the telephone? In any event, he wasted no time with unnecessary words, didn't ask Galloway how he was.

"I've fixed an interview with your son for three o'clock this afternoon at the District Attorney's office. Be in the entrance hall a few minutes earlier, and I'll meet you there."

Lane hung up without giving him time to ask any questions. Musselman was like that, even when he had nothing to do, just to make himself look busy. Galloway went down to the restaurant for lunch, reached the Police Court long before the time, walked up and down, then began to read all the administrative announcements on the notice boards.

The lawyer arrived at two minutes to three and, without stopping, motioned to him to follow him down a long corridor.

"The interview will take place in the presence of the District Attorney," he said as they went.

"Did he insist on that?"

"No. Your son did."

"You've spoken to him?"

"For half an hour, early this morning, and I came around later to be present at his interrogation."

What had been said, the way Ben had reacted, was apparently not his business, since he was told nothing about it.

Lane knocked at the door, opened it without awaiting a reply, and touched his pearl-gray hat as he passed through a room where two secretaries were working.

"They're there?" he asked in the manner of a regular visitor.

He pushed open the second door and Ben was there, in the middle of the room, seated in a chair with his legs crossed, smoking a cigarette. The District Attorney sat facing him, on the other side of his desk. He was a man of about forty who did not look in the best of health and was worried—overconscientious, probably.

"Come in, Mr. Galloway," he said, standing up.

Ben did the same, turning toward him:

"Hello, Dad."

He said it nicely, but without feeling, as he did, for example, when he came home from high school. They did not approach one another. Embarrassed by the presence of the two men, who pretended to be talking in low voices in a corner, Dave could find nothing to say. Perhaps he would have been equally at a loss if he had been alone with his son?

He finally murmured:

"Did you hear my message?"

He had seldom seen in Ben an attitude so casual. He seemed, in two days, to have rid himself of all the shyness and uncouthness of the awkward age, bore himself naturally, without constraint.

"To tell you the truth, it never occurred to us to turn on the radio, but I read it yesterday on the plane."

He made no comment on what his father had said. Everyone had pictured the fugitives hanging on the radio in the hope of guessing the police plans. As Ben said with simplicity, the thought had not occurred to them. And he added with an amused smile:

"It was the same with the route we took. They were looking for us on the side roads when, except the two times we got lost, we drove along the highway."

He was silent; Dave for his part remained speechless, gazing with avid eyes at his son, who had slightly turned his head away and he saw him now in profile. He noted that Ben had shaved and wore a clean shirt.

"You know, Dad, you'd do better to go back to Everton. They don't know yet when we'll go before the jury. That depends on the psychiatrists, who are due from New York tomorrow."

He was referring to the jury and the psychiatrists without a trace of embarrassment.

"If you see Jimmy Van Horn, tell him I'm sorry for his sake. I didn't give the show away."

"You haven't anything to say to me, myself, Ben?"

He was almost begging. His son replied:

"What do you want me to say? Anything I might say would only hurt you. Go back to Everton. Don't worry about me. I don't regret anything and, if I had to do it over again, I'd do exactly the same."

He turned toward the District Attorney.

"Will that do?" he asked, as though he had only consented to see his father at the magistrate's persuasion.

The District Attorney was not at ease and would undoubtedly have preferred not to be landed with an affair that was being discussed in every newspaper in the United States.

"It seems he has nothing more to say to you, Mr. Galloway."

He added after a pause, as though to avoid the appearance of turning him out too brutally:

"It's quite true we can't fix a date for the Grand Jury until after the psychiatrists have reached their conclusions."

Ben leaned forward to put out his cigarette in the ash tray.

"So long, Dad," he murmured, to induce his father to go.

"So long, Son."

Lane followed him out. Dave did not remember having taken leave of the District Attorney and nearly went back to apologize.

"The way you've just seen him, that's the way he was with me this morning and, afterwards, at his interrogation."

The lawyer spoke angrily, as though he were accusing Galloway of being responsible.

"There was a chance, at a pinch, we could deny premeditation and claim that the idea of attacking a motorist only occurred to him after he was on the road."

Dave had no sense of listening; he was surrounded, as it were, by a zone of emptiness that protected him.

"He insisted, on the contrary, on telling the District Attorney that he had made his plans in detail three weeks earlier. He chose a Saturday, it seems, because that's the day you go and spend the evening with a neighbor. Actually, the start, fixed for the previous Saturday, had to be postponed because you had a cold and didn't leave the apartment. Is that correct?"

"That's correct."

"Lillian Hawkins' lawyer is doing no better with her. Your son tried again to take everything on himself. According to her, she not only worked out the whole plan with him, but it was she who took the initiative. It was also she, in the Oldsmobile, who signaled to Ben when it was time to fire."

He was in a bad temper.

"The thing I don't understand is that you've lived sixteen years with a boy like him without noticing anything."

Dave almost wanted to ask his forgiveness. What could he do? So much the better if they blamed him, if the whole world blamed him. It was no more than justice that he should be held responsible.

"Do you intend to take his advice?"

"What advice?"

"To go back to Everton."

He shook his head. He would stay near Ben to the end, even if he could only see him at a distance and from time to time.

"As you please. The psychiatrist I have selected is Dr. Hassberger, who will be here tomorrow morning at the same time as the expert called in by the District Attorney. As things are now, I must warn you not to expect miracles."

Galloway saw him again, standing there in the half light of the corridor, in his blue suit, with his silky white hair. Finally Lane touched him on the shoulder with a protective gesture.

"Go and get some rest. Stay in your room in case I need you."

It was a room with twin beds. The tinted wallpaper had wide vertical stripes, dark green on light green, and one of the springs in the armchair protruded slightly. Dave spent the best part of his time at the window, watching the comings and goings around the Police Court, but either Ben was not taken there, or he was taken in and out by a back door. On the other hand, he saw Wilbur Lane come out, at about five, in company with one of the secretaries he had seen in the District Attorney's office.

After dinner he again nearly telephoned Musak, but lacked the courage. Lane was angry with him; he wondered why. As for the District Attorney, he was uncomfortable in his presence.

He fell alseep finally, was surprised, when he awoke, to find that it was eight in the morning. Until ten he waited for some word from the lawyer and, unable to bear it any longer, called him at his office. Lane was a long time coming to the phone and, while he talked, he seemed to be listening to what some visitor was saying.

"I promised to call you if I had any news. I've nothing to tell you at present. . . . No. . . . Dr. Hassberger arrived at eight, and since then he has been examining your son at the jail. . . . That's right. . . . I'll call you. . . ."

At midday he had still not been called. Not until one o'clock did the telephone ring.

"The case will go before the Grand Jury at ten o'clock Thursday morning," Lane snapped almost brutally.

"That means?"

"That means that Hassberger has found him sound in body and mind and a hundred per cent responsible for his actions. If that's our expert's opinion, we can't hope for anything better from the prosecution expert. I shall probably call you as a witness, and in that case I'll have to talk to you, probably sometime this afternoon."

He gave no further sign of life. Dave remained without news and at about half-past four ended by going to the lawyer's office. It served no purpose. The secretary told him that Lane was in conference and could not see him.

Galloway was surprised, not merely at not suffering any more, but that he should have become insensible to petty vexations of this kind. Since he had had nothing to do, time had ceased to count; he passed hours in the armchair in his room, or at the window, and the chambermaid had to take advantage of mealtimes to come in and clean.

At a certain moment there was a knock on the door and a stranger, who looked like a policeman in plain clothes, handed him a summons to appear as a witness before the Grand Jury on the following day.

He arrived at the Police Court half an hour early and it appeared to him that Wilbur Lane, who was talking in a group of people, pretended not to see him.

About thirty people only, mostly women, were seated on the light-colored benches in the courtroom, and the rest strolled up and down the corridor or chatted in corners smoking cigarettes.

He saw Dr. Van Horn with Jimmy, but Van Horn turned his back on him and went toward the lawyer, with whom he talked familiarly as though they had known one another a long time. Isabel Hawkins was there too, accompanied, this time, by her son Steve, and neither of them greeted him.

A young reporter asked him, almost gaily:

"Excited?"

He could only give him a forced smile. He was hoping to see his son's arrival, not knowing that for the past half hour he had been in the District Attorney's office.

A few moments before the usher came along the corridor ringing his bell Lane seemed to become aware of his presence.

"I had you subpoenaed just in case. I shall ask you two or three unimportant questions. It's even possible I shan't call you at all. In any case, don't get impatient."

"Won't I be in the courtroom?"

"Not until you've testified."

Hadn't Lane caused him to be subpoenaed deliberately, in order to be relieved of him during the proceedings? They called the witnesses and showed them into a room flanked by backed benches where there were copper spittoons and a drinking fountain with paper cups. The lieutenant who had questioned him on Sunday morning was there, freshly shaven, and gave him a warm handshake. Isabel Hawkins was seated on one of the benches accompanied by her son Steve, who was talking in an undertone to Jimmy Van Horn.

There were other people he did not know, in particular a woman of about forty, dressed in black, whose eyes he often felt fixed upon him.

It was not the lieutenant, but another patrolman in uniform, who was first sent for, no doubt the one who had found the car at the side of the road. They could not hear what was being said in the next room, because there was a padded inner door, but they sometimes caught a murmur of voices and, more clearly, the tap of the presiding judge's gavel on the desk.

A second policeman passed through the door to the courtroom, then at length the lieutenant, who stayed longer than the two others. After they had testified, they didn't return. Perhaps they remained in court. Perhaps they went away? Dave didn't know what happened, because he had never in his life been at an indictment. A little earlier, in the corridor, he had heard someone who looked important say that it would be over very quickly, that it was really no more than a formality, since the youngsters did not deny anything.

The fourth witness looked like a doctor, probably the one who had examined the body of Charles Ralston.

If Galloway understood rightly, they were engaged in establishing the facts from successive testimonies. It was the woman in mourning who was next called, after which the hearing was adjourned and footsteps were heard in the corridor where everyone hurried in order to smoke. The witnesses themselves were not allowed to leave the room and there was a policeman, seated by the door, to prevent their doing so.

When the usher reappeared, Isabel Hawkins half rose, thinking it was her turn, but it was to Galloway that he beckoned.

The courtroom was very much brighter than the little room he had left, and because of the heat they had opened the two big windows giving onto the park, so that one heard the noises from outside. Between a hundred and a hundred and fifty people were seated on the benches and he recognized the Everton garageman, the hairdresser, and even old Mrs. Pinch. The garageman alone raised his hand in greeting.

Not until he turned around did he discover the judge, alone at his desk, on a sort of dais at the foot of which the District Attorney and his assistants were seated at the same table as the press reporters.

Ben was seated on a bench, to the left, facing the jury, with Lillian beside him, and the two of them, attentively following what went on in the court, occasionally leaned toward one another to exchange a remark when they recognized a new face.

Galloway raised his hand, repeated:

"I do."

After which he was made to sit down facing the jury and the public and Lane advanced toward him.

"First of all I should like the witness to tell us his son's age when Mrs. Galloway left their home. Answer, please."

"Six months."

"Since then, your son has never left you?"

"Never."

"There has never been any question of your remarrying?"

"No, sir."

"You have no sister, no woman relative of any degree living with you in your home or visiting it regularly?"

He thought he saw an amused smile on Ben's lips, as though he could see what the lawyer was driving at.

"You have no maid, either?"

He shook his head.

"Did friends visit your home with their wives?"

He could still only answer in the negative, and Ben was not the only one to smile, others in the courtroom were amused at his embarrassment.

"If I understand you rightly, your son passed his childhood, then part of his adolescence, without ever seeing a woman in his home?"

It was the first time this had ever struck him.

"It's quite true. Except the help, two days a week."

He corrected himself.

"But no! Now that I come to think of it, Ben was at school at the times she came to work."

There was a burst of laughter and the judge used his gavel. He was a middle-aged man of insignificant appearance.

"Thank you, Mr. Galloway," said Lane.

He turned to the District Attorney.

"If you wish to cross-examine my witness . . ."

Temple hesitated, consulted a young man on his left.

"Just one question. On Saturday, May 7, that is to say, a week ago last Saturday, was the witness prevented by a cold from visiting a friend as he is in the habit of doing every Saturday?"

"Quite correct."

"That's all," murmured the District Attorney, writing a few words on a sheet of paper.

Dave did not know what to do, wondered whether he should leave and, seeing an empty place on the front bench, went and sat there.

He was just opposite his son, within five yards of him. Without Ben's appearing to act deliberately he never turned his head his way and not once did their eyes meet.

It was not he who counted in Ben's eyes, but Lillian, at whom he smiled from time to time, perhaps also the people who were watching them.

All the time the session lasted Dave sought in vain to attract his attention, going as far as to cough so loudly that the judge gave him a look of reproof.

It was important that Ben should look at him, because then he would realize the transformation that had taken place in him. He was not tense; his face was serene. He wore on his lips a faint smile resembling his son's smile. It was like a message that Ben continued not to see.

Isabel Hawkins had taken her place on the chair Galloway had just left, her handbag on her knees, and Cavanaugh moved forward to question her, very much more simply than Lane had done.

"How long have your daughter and Ben Galloway been seeing each other regularly?"

She answered in a low voice:

"So far as I know, it would be about three months."

"Speak up!" said someone on the public benches.

She repeated loudly:

"So far as I know, it would be about three months."

"He came regularly to your house?"

"He used to come long before that, because of my son Steve, but he didn't take any notice of my daughter."

"What happened last Saturday?"

"You know quite well. She ran away with him."

"Did you see her go?"

"If I'd seen her I wouldn't have let her go."

"Did you not then pay a certain visit?"

"I went to the Galloways' house, because I was afraid my husband would do something silly if I let him go alone."

"Did Mr. Galloway know that his son had run away with Lillian?"

"He knew his son had gone, but he didn't know who with."

"Did he seem surprised?"

"I can't say he did."

There must have been other questions, but Dave did not listen to them; he still wore on his face the sort of message he was trying vainly to communicate to his son.

It was the District Attorney who asked, in the course of cross-examination:

"After finding that your daughter had gone, did you not make a second discovery?"

"My husband's pay was no longer in the box."

Then came the turn of Jimmy Van Horn, who looked around the room for his father and invariably replied:

"Yes, Your Honor. . . . No, Your Honor. . . . Yes, Your Honor. . . ."

One day when Ben had been at their house, he had shown him the doctor's automatic and Ben had asked him to sell it to him.

"He paid you five dollars for it?"

"Yes, Your Honor."

"Did he give you the money?"

"No, Your Honor, only three. He was to give me the other two the next week."

Again there was laughter. The members of the jury, for the most part, held themselves as rigid and immobile as in a family photograph and there were two women among them.

Galloway did not at once understand why the judge rose and put on his cap, muttering unintelligible words as he did so. It seemed that the hearing was adjourned, this time for an hour to enable everyone to have lunch. Only the members of the jury and the witnesses who had not yet been called were not allowed to leave.

"I suppose," his lawyer came and said to him, "it would be no use asking you not to come to the afternoon session?"

He merely shook his head. Why shouldn't he be present, when there was still a chance of seeing Ben and being near him?

"The two psychiatrists are going to testify. If they don't take too long, there's a chance that the District Attorney will make his speech for the prosecution today and even that I may make my defense, in which case everything may be over by this evening."

Dave did not react. He had come to view what was happening around him as though it did not concern him personally. Since his son had been taken out of the courtroom, he didn't stay there either, but went and had a sandwich in a restaurant resembling Mack's Lunch. Nearly everyone was there, but no one took any notice of him; only the Everton garageman came and shook him by the hand saying:

"My, but it's hot in there!"

One of the psychiatrists was old, with a foreign accent, the other middle-aged, and Wilbur Lane made a great display, questioning them, using their own jargon, with which he seemed to be familiar.

Several times Dave felt the judge's eyes rest upon him; perhaps it was accidental: having to sit facing the crowd for hours on end, he was bound to look somewhere.

There was another adjournment, of only a few minutes, during which Ben and Lillian remained in the courtroom. Isabel Hawkins took advantage of it to go and talk to her daughter and the policeman allowed her to do so. Dave himself did not venture to approach his son, for fear of displeasing him. He longed with all his heart for Ben to look at him and see the distance he had traveled.

The District Attorney spoke for twenty minutes, in a monotonous voice, after which it was the turn of Cavanaugh, who was even more brief, and finally of Wilbur Lane.

The jury was absent not more than half an hour, and shortly before their return Ben and Lillian were brought back, seeming still quite at ease; the girl even waved to someone she recognized among the public.

Less than five minutes later it was over. The jury had unanimously decided to indict Ben Galloway of murder in the first degree, Lillian Hawkins of complicity.

Dave watched his son's face so intensely during the reading of the verdict that it made his eyes ache. He was almost sure he saw a slight quivering of the lips and nostrils, then, instantly, Ben recovered his smile and turned to Lillian, who smiled back at him.

He did not look at his father. In the confusion that followed the latter tried in vain to thrust himself into his field of vision, lost sight of him, heard a voice, that of Lane, saying to him resentfully:

"I did everything that was humanly possible. It was he who wanted it that way."

Galloway bore him no grudge. He didn't like him, any more than he'd liked Musselman, but he had nothing special against him.

"Thank you for everything," he said to the lawyer politely.

The latter, surprised at finding him so submissive, went on:

"The trial won't begin for another month, and maybe between now and then something will turn up."

Dave did not know that as he shook the lawyer's hand he was smiling at him with almost the same smile that his son had had on his lips all day.

The sun was shining outside and the garageman was driving the hairdresser and old Mrs. Pinch away in his car.

9

He reopened his shop two days later at the usual time, and on Saturday went to Musak's house, spoke of nothing, watched at a distance the baseball players in the setting sun, then played his game of backgammon with the cabinetmaker, who smoked his mended pipe.

Widowers, in the beginning, must have the same sensation that he had during the first days, when he sometimes turned around to speak to Ben, or when, at certain times of day, he glanced impatiently at the clock, thinking his son was late; once at least, in the morning, he found himself breaking eggs for two into the pan.

This soon passed, however. Ben was always there, not only in their apartment, but in the shop, in the streets, everywhere he went, and Galloway no longer so greatly needed his physical presence.

Perhaps the travail that had taken place in him had begun before the session of the Grand Jury, or on the Saturday night, for example, when, seated in his green armchair, he had still awaited Ben's return without much believing in it. Or perhaps even before that?

He had spent his life watching his son, and until the moment when he saw him before the court, carefree, a smile on his lips, he had not understood.

One weekday morning he hung the sign on his glass-paneled door and went to call on Musak, who was in his workshop. Almost blushing, as though he feared to betray his deepest secret, he took three photographs out of an envelope.

"I'd like you to make me a single frame for the three of them," he said, arranging them in a certain order on the bench. "A very simple frame, just a rim of unstained wood."

The first was a picture of his father, at about the age of thirty-eight, exactly as Dave remembered him, with his mustache emphasizing his slightly mocking expression. The second was a photograph of himself, when he was twenty-two and had just entered the works at Waterbury. His neck looked longer and thinner than now. He had his head in half profile and the corner of his mouth was slightly drawn in.

The last photograph was the one of Ben that a school friend had taken a month ago. He, too, had a long neck and it was the first time he had been photographed smoking a cigarette.

Musak brought him the frame the same day toward the end of the afternoon and Dave at once hung it on the wall. It seemed to him that those three photographs contained the explanation of everything that had happened, but he realized that he alone could understand and that, if he tried to communicate his feeling to any other person, to Wilbur Lane, for example, he would be stared at in consternation.

Didn't the gaze of the three men reveal a shared secret life, a life, rather, that had been made to recoil upon itself? A look of timidity, almost a look of resignation, while the identical drawing in of the lips hinted at a suppressed revolt.

They were of the same breed, all three of them, the breed opposed to that of a Lane, or of a Musselman, or of his mother. It seemed to him that, in the whole world, there were only two sorts of men, those who bow their heads and the others. As a child, he had already thought it in more literal terms: the whipped and those who whip.

His father had bowed his head, spent his life soliciting loans from the banks, and it was while he was once again waiting in a banker's anteroom that he had died. Had not that irony of fate caused him to smile at the last moment?

Once only in his life had he accomplished an act that might pass for a revolt, and subsequently he had been made every day to pay for it; years later Dave's mother was still using the incident to besmirch his memory, saying to her son:

"You'll never be anything but a Galloway!"

It had happened before Dave was born. No one, except his father, knew exactly what had taken place. One Fourth of July night he had simply not come home. His mother had telephoned his club, and various friends, without obtaining news of him, and he had not returned until the following day at eight in the morning. He had tried in vain to get to his room without being seen, just as he had tried to remove the traces of lipstick from his shirt collar.

He had listened all his life to reproaches for this escapade, and each time he bowed his head. Dave was nonetheless convinced that he was glad he had done it. Sometimes, when his wife spoke harshly to him, the father winked at his son, as though the child were already able to understand.

Wasn't it for the same reason that every day he drank a certain quantity of bourbon, never enough to make him drunk, but sufficient to dull the edge of reality?

Dave had never drunk. He had fitted his life to his own measure, which he knew well, but he, too, had made his revolt, going a stage further in violence than his father. When he had married Ruth, he had performed an act of defiance; he didn't know precisely of what or of whom, defiance of the world, of all the Musselmans, all the Lanes on earth.

He had deliberately chosen her for what she was, and if he had found a girl on the streets he would doubtless have preferred her.

He might one day tell Ben of his father's revolt in Virginia, but he could not, alas, tell him of his own. Who knows? Perhaps his son would come to understand of his own accord?

What Dave looked for in Ben's eyes, even when he was still a child, was perhaps a hint, a sign of that revolt. In those days he was afraid of it. He could almost have wished that his son were of the other breed.

But Ben had the same look, that of his father and himself, of all the others who resembled them. Some were able all their lives to prevent their revolt from coming to the surface. With others it breaks out.

The two psychiatrists had discussed Ben without knowing that once in his life his grandfather had spent the night out, and that his father had married a slut who had been had by all his friends. Ben, at sixteen, had felt the need to make an end.

It was not without reason that Dave had put the three photographs in the same frame. The three men stood together. Each was in some way no more than a stage in one single process of evolution.

Even before, it was rare for Dave to pass a whole day without thinking of his father. Now he was nearly as much present in the house as Ben.

His mother had not written, had not come to see him. She must certainly have read the story in the papers. She must have said to Musselman:

"I always prophesied that would end badly!"

It was true. Wilbur Lane, too, had at once predicted that Ben would be indicted. Those people are invariably right.

From then on it was a little as though the cycle were complete. Dave worked as usual, opened and closed the shop with the same meticulous movements, moved the watches and jewels from the display window into the safe for the night, did his shopping at the First National Store, and went upstairs to prepare his meals.

The people in the village had already ceased to look curiously at him. It was he who sometimes surprised them, who shocked them perhaps, by talking to them of Ben as though nothing had happened. Ben was with him, within him, all day long, no matter where he went.

The month passed without a drop of rain and the men went about without jackets. The police had brought back his car, which he used when necessary.

Wilbur Lane spent a day in Everton, questioning school-teachers, Ben's friends, shop people, but he saw Dave only briefly.

"The trial's fixed for next Tuesday."

"How's Ben?"

The lawyer's face darkened.

"The same as ever, unfortunately!"

This occasion was much more important than the first, and the hearing lasted three days, during which Dave occupied the same room at the hotel, with light and dark green stripes. The hotel was full. Reporters had come in great numbers from New York and elsewhere, not only with press photographers, but with movie and television cameramen. The judge, at the first session, ordered that no camera was to be allowed in the courtroom and one saw them everywhere in the hall, in the corridors, even in the lobby of the hotel, where most of the witnesses were staying.

Ben had not grown thinner, if anything was a little less angular. All the first day his father remained shut in the witness room, as the first time. He had resolved, if he had the chance, to try to explain, if only for Ben's benefit, what he had discovered. Not necessarily everything, but the essentials, and he was careful to say nothing of this to Lane.

The lawyer evidently mistrusted him, because he asked him only a few unimportant questions, cutting him short when he threatened to say more.

All he managed to say, thrown in hastily when he was about to leave the witness stand, was:

"My son and I stand together."

There was no one to understand. He even had the impression that his words had caused embarrassment, as though he had been guilty of a solecism.

When he looked at Ben a little later, he had the conviction that he had not understood either. Several times, during the trial, his son glanced curiously at him. He was no longer seated beside Lillian, as on the first occasion, because they had been separated. The proceedings took place in a large room, with greater solemnity, but during the adjournments the people were in no less of a hurry to go out and smoke or drink a Coca-Cola.

On the last day he recognized more than thirty Everton people who had come by bus, and the door was left open to allow the spectators crowding the corridors to hear.

A place was kept for him, always the same place, in the second row, between a young lawyer from Poughkeepsie and the wife of one of the judges. Wilbur Lane spoke for two and a half hours and the jury withdrew to deliberate shortly before five in the afternoon.

Everyone, or nearly everyone, left the courtroom. At six o'clock, at seven, the stone steps at the foot of the white columns of the court were still crowded with people and the men returning from a nearby bar smelled of liquor.

Some made little signs of recognition to Dave as they passed near him. Others must have been astonished to find him so calm. He knew they would not dare to kill his son. Later, as he had the right to do, he would visit him in prison, and little by little, without trying to go too fast, he would manage to make Ben understand that they were one. Hadn't he himself taken years to make the discovery?

The street lights went on together in the dusk, the neon signs shone on either side of Main Street, insects began to buzz around heads. People who were in the know, and went from time to time to get the latest news, came back and said to the others:

"They still can't manage to agree, particularly about the girl."

At half-past ten, at last, there was a movement in the crowd and everyone converged on the courtroom. In the artificial light it made one think more than ever of a Methodist church or a lecture hall.

Ben's and Lillian's places remained empty for nearly a quarter of an hour and, when they were brought in, Dave thought both their faces seemed drawn, perhaps, in part, because of the lighting.

The judge entered, then the jury. The foreman of the jury rose in an absolute silence, a sheet of paper in his hand, to read the verdict.

" 'The hereinafter-named, Ben Galloway, sixteen years, and Lillian Hawkins, fifteen years and a half, both of Everton, in the state of New York, were convicted of murder in the first degree and sentenced to death. In view of their ages, however, the jury recommended that the sentence be commuted to imprisonment for life.' "

From someone on the benches came a sob that resembled a cry. It was Isabel Hawkins, whose husband, now sober, dressed as though for a wedding, accompanied her.

Was it his father Ben sought with his gaze at the moment when they were preparing to take him away? In any event their eyes met and Ben's lip quivered, was drawn in on one side only, as in the three photographs.

Dave strove to put into his eyes all that was in him, to pour his spirit into his son, who finally disappeared through a small varnished door.

He had had no time to observe Lillian.

The papers and the radio announced a few days later that Ben Galloway had been taken to Sing Sing while the girl had been sent to a women's penitentiary.

Then he received a letter from Wilbur Lane, notifying him of the total amount of his fees and expenses and informing him that he was entitled to write his son a letter every two weeks and, if the latter's conduct were good, to visit him once a month.

It was quite near, scarcely twenty-three miles, on the banks of the Hudson. He paid Lane and there remained to him almost none of his savings. This no longer mattered. Indeed it was better so. What could he have done with the money?

The first visit was the most sterile, because Ben had grown no tamer, continued to regard his father as though they were not both of the same kind.

Dave would take as much time as was needed to make him understand that each of the three had had his revolt, that each of the three was responsible, and that, outside prison, he was paying the same price as his son.

Hadn't all three imagined that they were going to set themselves free?

"You're eating well?" he asked.

"Not badly."

"The food isn't too bad?"

It wasn't the words that mattered. These, like the "Yes, sir" of the colored man in the Virginia sunshine, were in some sort no more than incantations.

"Is the work hard?"

They had put Ben in a bookbinding shop and his fingers were covered with cuts, some of which seemed to be inflamed.

At the end of the second month the papers suddenly revived the affair to announce that Lillian Hawkins was pregnant and would be transferred at the appropriate time to another penitentiary where she could keep the baby.

When Dave next saw his son, the boy did not speak to him of this, but more than ever he had the resigned and melancholy look of the Galloways, with, somewhere, for those who could see, a little secret flame.

Who knows? Now that Fate had been conjured, perhaps it was a different cycle that was about to begin?

Often, in his apartment, in his shop, and even in the street, Dave talked in a low voice to his father and to his son, who went with him everywhere. Soon he would talk to his grandson as well to reveal to him the secret in men.

Shadow Rock Farm
Lakeville, Connecticut
March 24, 1954